SUSETTE'S AWESOME ADVENTURE

When I fully came to, Tommy was kneeling beside me.

"Sus, are you okay?"

I nodded. "Thank you," I whispered.

He shook his head and smiled. "I couldn't exactly let you drown, could I? The only problem is, spinning out of that whirlpool, you and I crashed into a rock pretty hard. I took most of the blow and cracked my wrist."

I could tell by the unnatural angle of his wrist and the way it had already swelled that it was probably broken.

"Could you take off your T-shirt?" I asked quickly.

I took his T-shirt to the river and soaked it. Then I carefully wrapped the cold cloth once around his hand and wrist and tied it around his chest to keep the wrist stable.

"It's like a splint," I said. "It will immobilize your wrist till a doctor can take a look at it. Hopefully the cold water will keep it from swelling too much more."

He looked down at his makeshift splint. "You're as smart as I thought you were."

I blushed. "S-so now what?"

"We get back into the water and swim downstream to the raft," Tommy said simply.

That was when it dawned on me. After an experience so terrifying it had almost made my heart stop, he actually expected me to get back in the river and go through it again. Well, I had one answer for that.

"No," I said out loud.

#2: Susette's Awesome Adventure

Mallory Tarcher

Z·FAVE
KENSINGTON PUBLISHING CORP.

Z*FAVE BOOKS are published by

Kensington Publishing Corp.
850 Third Avenue
New York, NY 10022

First Printing: September, 1994

Printed in the United States of America

To Ann,
with love, thanks, and admiration

You gain strength, courage, and confidence by every experience in which you really stop to look fear in the face. . . . You must do the thing you think you cannot do.

—Eleanor Roosevelt

One

Dear Mom,

Yahooo! We're off on trip number two. Grand Canyon, here we come!

I promise, I really, really do, that I will not get into trouble on this one. No skydiving, no lost gold mines, no nothing. I'll be sweet and patient and I'll do what Debbie says.

Okay. Fine. Would you believe I won't get into as *much* trouble? I'll try to do *most* of what Debbie says?

Gotta go. The stewardess is coming with her drink cart. If I smile really nicely, she'll give me a whole can of Coke.

I'll write soon. Thanks for planning the best summer of my whole life.

Love,
Toni

* * *

Dear Robbie,

Toni keeps trying to get me to listen to this lame song on her Walkman, so I figured if I wrote a letter, she'd leave me alone. We're on our way to the Grand Canyon. I can't wait. I'll try to catch a lizard for you. Oh, and will you tell Mom to send my windbreaker? I forgot it.

I'll write again soon. Don't start working on the transmission without me. Please, please, please.

Don't let them work you too hard at Dad's office. And tell Vince and Michael to STAY OUT of my room or I will KILL them.

Love,
Allison

Dear Cassie,

How's camp? I already miss it sooo much. How does it feel to finally be a C.I.T.? Which horse are you riding this year?

We're off on our second trip. This one's to the Grand Canyon. I still can't believe I'm doing this. If this trip is anything like the last one, please ask Ms. Wecker to save a bunk for me in cabin six, okay? Just kidding. Vancouver was fun, but I really don't like getting caught in storms and sleeping in mine shafts. Anyway, the Grand Canyon should be a breeze.

Write me soon. Tell Brittany and Hannah I say hi.

Love,
Rosina

Dear Grandpa,

I miss you already. Thank you a million times for talking Mom and Papa into letting me go this summer. It's the most incredible adventure of my whole life. *Please* tell them not to worry about anything. (The whole gold-mine thing in Vancouver is still our secret, right?)

I'm so excited to see the Grand Canyon. I'm going to take a photograph of it in my memory and describe it to you perfectly. You're going to feel like you could see it yourself.

And I'm not going to worry about the thing we talked about.

I love you, Grandpa. Write me soon.

Susette

* * *

I looked up from my letter to see Toni Francis giggling with Allison Morris and pointing to the flight attendant shuttling down the skinny airplane aisle with a big silver cart full of sodas. Suddenly I realized what they were looking at, and I had to stifle a laugh. The perfectly dressed flight attendant with that perfect hair-sprayed helmet of hair had a napkin stuck to her butt. I blushed. I couldn't help it.

Toni saw that she'd caught my eye and started laughing even harder. I slapped my hand over my mouth and sat back in my seat.

I haven't known Toni that long, but she's already becoming one of my best friends. She's small and thin and has long curly brown hair. She has big green eyes, a few freckles on her slightly upturned nose, and she gets this devilish gleam in her eye when she's doing something she shouldn't, which is pretty often. She's really cute, although she'd probably kick you in the shin if you called her that. She's a little touchy about being small. The other thing she's touchy about is her real name—Antoinette. I think it's really romantic. She says it makes her want to hurl.

She and I are pretty much opposites. Toni is very outgoing. She's not afraid of anything or anyone. She never thinks before she opens her mouth. I, on the other hand, think a lot before I open my mouth, which means sometimes I don't say very much.

Allison and I are getting to be good friends, too. Allison and Toni are best friends from way back. They know each other so well, they can practically read each other's minds. Allison is taller and more, um . . . developed than me or Toni. She's African-American and has gorgeous long black hair, sort of like Janet Jackson's. Don't you hate people who always have perfect hair? I'm not one of those people. I not only have bad-hair days, I have bad-hair *years*. Anyway, Allison loves to laugh at the crazy things Toni does, but she's a lot more laid back. She's very cool, very down to earth. She also knows a lot more about boys than, say, I do. She has five, yes count 'em, *five* brothers. She's a perfectionist and a genius mechanic according to Mrs. Francis, whose muffler she repaired a couple of weeks ago just for the fun of it. I've never thought of mufflers as fun, but hey.

Rosina Iglesias was sitting next to me taking a quiz in *Sassy* magazine. She looked up and rolled her eyes at Toni. I know she thought they were being really immature. Rosina, like Allison and Toni, is fourteen. She has long, light brown hair, blue eyes and delicate features. Rosina is a lot harder to get to know than the other two. She can be kind of spoiled and prissy sometimes. I think that's partly because she's an only child and her parents are rich. She's the only one of us who doesn't always seem totally psyched to be spending her summer this way. But down deep, I think she has a good heart.

My name is Susette Yoshi. My family is Japanese-American. I'm small, though not as small as Toni, and I have silky straight black hair and dark brown eyes. I can't tell you more, because . . . well, because it's impossible to try to describe yourself.

You're probably wondering what I was doing on an airplane with four other ninth-graders from Santa Barbara, California. Well, I'm glad you asked. It's an amazing story.

Last spring an anonymous grant was given to the Santa Barbara Women's Council to "broaden the horizons of young girls." The council decided to send four girls and a teacher around the world for the summer. Every girl in our eighth-grade class was invited to submit an essay, and Mr. McGonigle, the most popular teacher in the high school, along with the council members *without* daughters who were contestants, chose four of them.

You guessed it—Toni, Allison, Rosina, and I were the lucky winners.

And Mr. McGonigle, now known as John, is the not-so-lucky teacher stuck with us for the summer. He's young and cool (and very cute, I must admit), as teachers go. In fact, at this moment he was sitting in the seat behind mine blasting Pearl Jam on his Walkman.

Sitting next to John was Debbie Francis, Toni's older sister. Debbie is eighteen and very nice. Mrs. Francis, Toni and Debbie's mom, runs a travel agency called Adventures Inc. which helped plan our trip, and she sent Debbie to be John's assistant. Debbie is tallish and thin, with long wavy strawberry-blond hair. She has those perfect California looks that make somebody like me, who's not very tall and has kind of unusual Japanese-American looks, feel a little insecure. She can be bossy and uptight sometimes. But she has a big, wonderful laugh that just gets away from her. That alone keeps her from being too serious. I should probably mention that Debbie has a massive crush on John.

So we'd all flown early this morning from Santa Barbara to Las Vegas, where we'd connected with a little plane to take us to Grand

Canyon Airport, right on the rim of the Grand Canyon.

This was our second big trip of the summer. Our first trip was to Vancouver, and we had the most unbelievably incredible time. We loved Vancouver, but the adventure really started when we went hiking on Whistler Mountain. Toni managed to talk us into searching for a gold mine. I have to admit, I got kind of excited about it, too. See, we met this guy named Paul and his grandpa George on the mountain. I really, really liked Grandpa George—I guess he reminded me of my own grandpa—and finding the gold mine was Grandpa George's lifelong dream. He and Paul had spent five summers searching for it, and he wasn't feeling strong enough to look much longer. So we decided that with the four of us and Paul, there was no way we could lose.

I'll give you the quick version of the story: we got stuck there in an incredible thunderstorm with hurricane-force winds, spent the night in the mine shaft, and were rescued when Toni and Ranger Magee parachuted in after us. It was scary, but the most thrilling experience of my life. If my parents had found out what we did, they would have locked me in my room for the rest of my life.

Which is why I kind of didn't tell them. I did tell my grandpa, though. He made me promise that we'd be more careful, but I could tell he was proud of us for being so brave. I just knew he'd understand.

Now we were making our way across the U.S., first to the Grand Canyon, and then after that to Maine. If our first trip was any clue, we were going to have a blast.

"Ladies and gentleman," the captain's voice came over the P.A. system. "If you'll look out of the right side of the airplane, you'll see a magnificent view of the Grand Canyon."

I leaned across Rosina and stared out the window. It was incredible. From the sky the Grand Canyon is this huge scar in the earth, like a big, long crater. At the bottom I could make out a silvery river snaking through the canyon. The late-afternoon sun turned the land a deep orangey-pink color. It was one of the most beautiful sights I've ever seen.

I felt a chill of excitement skate up my spine. I knew we were in for another great adventure.

"Rosina, hurry up, would you?" Toni shouted down the long, gray-carpeted airport corridor.

At last we had landed at Grand Canyon Airport and gathered all of our luggage. Now we were trying to make it to the rental-car counter to pick up our car and drive to our hotel. We were all chugging along carrying our bags, and about twenty yards behind us was Rosina, trailing two of the biggest suitcases you've ever seen. Rosina has a thing for clothes. A big thing. She's one of those girls who kind of shocks you when she wears the same thing more than once.

"Okay, kids," John said once we'd all piled in to the bright red Jeep Cherokee we'd rented. (Very cool car. Since Ms. Francis planned this trip, she made sure we traveled in style.)

"Kids?" all four of us demanded at the same time.

John started laughing. "Girls? Young women? Sorry. I'm a slow learner." He put the key in the ignition, and the engine rumbled to life. "Listen, Debbie and I have a surprise planned for tomorrow. Instead of starting off tomorrow morning with the hike along the South Rim Nature Trail, we're going to do something different."

"Cool," Rosina piped in. "I hate hiking."

John gave her one of his don't-give-me-any-of-your-attitude looks. "Well I'm afraid you're out of luck, then. Because we *are* doing a rim-to-river hike first thing tomorrow morning."

"What's that?" Rosina asked suspiciously.

"It's where you follow one of the trails that start at the edge of the canyon and take you all the way to the Colorado River at the bottom," John explained.

Allison drew in her breath.

Rosina's mouth fell open.

I looked at John in surprise. I knew that this was a big deal, because I'd read a pamphlet about the Grand Canyon on the airplane. Believe it or not, the whole huge, incredible canyon was carved out over millions and millions of years by the Colorado River. It's over two hundred miles long and a mile deep. Pretty amazing to think a little river could sculpt out a canyon that big. Anyway, the only ways to get from the rim to the river at the bottom of the canyon are by foot and by mule. It's a long, steep trail with lots of switchbacks. You have to be brave and in very good shape to do it on foot.

"The reason we're heading down to the river right away," John explained, "is that one of Debbie's friends from high school, Jim Freeman, is working for the summer as a river guide for the Colorado River Rafting Company. He and Debbie will be taking you on a rafting trip through the rapids of the mighty Colorado the day after tomorrow. This is the opportunity of a lifetime, guys, so get psyched."

"Cool!" Toni squealed.

"Awesome!" Allison started applauding.

Even Rosina looked excited.

I just sat there staring at John. My stomach fell down into my high tops.

I wasn't happy at all. I was miserable. I had a sinking feeling that our rafting trip was going to be one of the worst experiences of my life.

Two

When I woke up the next morning, it took me a few seconds to remember where I was. I looked up at the ceiling of our hotel room, then across to the double bed, where Rosina was rolled up in the comforter.

It's funny the things you learn about people when you spend a few weeks sharing hotel rooms and beds. For example, all four of us have distinctive sleeping personalities: Rosina is a spooler. She rolls up in the comforter, so you find yourself shivering on the sheet when you share a bed with her. Toni is a wriggler. She always ends up horizontal across the mattress, and you have to wake her up in the middle of the night and make her get right-side-up again. I'm a buncher. I always curl up in a little ball and creep in tiny increments toward the middle of the bed. Allison is the one we all draw straws to sleep next to. She falls asleep on her back and *does not move*. We're all balled up, drooling, snoring, talking in our sleep, and Allison looks like a fashion model in a mattress ad.

I was lucky enough to have shared with Allison last night. She was still asleep next to me. I could hear the shower running in the bathroom—Toni, she was always the first up. I got out of bed and padded over to the big picture window. I drew the curtains and looked out across a scene that took my breath away.

Our hotel, the El Tovar, was perched right on the south rim of the canyon, and from our window you could see for miles and miles of buttes (which Toni insists on calling butts) and mesas.

The early morning sunlight transformed the canyon into a beautiful show of colors and textures. Every color imaginable was in the cliffs of the canyon—deep pink, purple, blue, yellow, magenta, peach.

I tried as hard as I could to think of a way of putting that sight into words. You see, my grandpa can't see very well, and I like to try to find ways to describe things to him. It's good practice for learning to be a writer, which is what I think I'd like to be someday.

Suddenly I felt something soft hit the back of my head. I turned around. Rosina's sock.

"Close the curtains, would you?" Rosina groaned.

I started to, and my eye caught sight of the Colorado River glinting in the sunlight. Suddenly my stomach was churning and my palms were moist. I remembered where we were going this morning and why.

"Okay, guys. Hold up," John said.

All six of us had assembled at the trailhead of the Bright Angel Trail, which we were taking down into the canyon. We were all wearing shorts, hiking boots, T-shirts, sweaters. Debbie was looking especially cool in her Ray-Bans. Toni had on her favorite San Francisco Giants baseball cap turned around backward on her head. Rosina was wearing fancy Italian hiking boots that she'd obviously never worn before in her life.

I was shivering, and my legs were covered with goosebumps, but John assured us it would be broiling hot at the bottom of the canyon.

"What are we waiting for?" Toni asked. Toni is so perky in the morning, you sometimes want to kill her.

"We're waiting for Tommy, our guide," John explained. "He's going to show us the way down the canyon and join you all rafting tomorrow."

I was conjuring up this image of a big, beefy park-ranger type, like Ranger Magee, who'd been our guide at Whistler, when this teenage guy taps John on the arm. This incredibly *cute* guy, probably about fourteen or fifteen, with thick, longish dark hair, burnished skin from spending lots of time outdoors, and a gorgeous smile.

"Tommy Tilousi?" John asked.

This was Tommy?

"Yeah. Hi. You must be John McGonigle."

John stuck out his hand. "Very nice to meet you."

John then introduced Tommy to all of us. I could tell Toni, Allison, and Rosina were just as surprised by Tommy's appearance as I was.

When John got around to introducing Tommy to me, I found myself blushing. I hate when I do that. I have to admit I don't have very much experience with guys. Okay, no experience with guys. My parents are really overprotective, you see, and they don't let me go to unsupervised parties, let alone on dates. I have twin sisters, age seven, and no brothers, so I'm just not very cool around guys. In fact, I'm a total dork around guys.

But had I just imagined it, or had Tommy's eyes rested on me for a second longer than necessary?

I just imagined it, I told myself as I slung my backpack over my shoulder and followed the group down the Bright Angel Trail.

Toni kept glancing at me, trying to get my attention. She was mouthing something.

"What?" I mouthed back.

"He's so *cute*."

I was so busy trying to read her lips, I tripped over my own two feet. How embarrassing.

Just over the edge of the canyon, we were met with another staggering view. I just stood there, soaking it in. I was transfixed by the endless vista of wavy walls and cliffs, overlapping and extending as far as the eye could see.

"Hey, move along, leadfoot."

My head snapped up and I looked around. It was Tommy, staring at me with a lopsided grin. My eyebrows shot up in astonishment. I opened my mouth, but no words came out. I shut it again. Instead of saying something cutting and witty in response to this obnoxious guy, I just sort of gurgled.

You know what really bothers me? The fact that cute guys always seem so full of themselves. As I said before, I'm no expert, but it seems like guys as cute as Tommy expect every single girl they meet to fall in love with them. Well, he was in for a disappointment.

"Go, go," he said. "We're supposed to make it to the bottom before the end of the summer."

I had no idea what to say. I tried to give him a withering stare, but I don't think it came out right. I just put down my head and started walking, hoping he wouldn't notice that my cheeks had turned a deep shade of red.

"Hey, Susie Q. Wait up, would you?"

Tommy again. I was seething. *Susie Q?* Nobody called me that. Who did this jerk think he was? I just walked faster. Typical arrogant guy. Yick.

By this point I was out ahead of the group, trying to enjoy the gorgeous views and trying to get away from Tommy, who seemed to be on a mission to make me miserable.

We had walked for four miles down, down, down. The colors of the canyon walls kept changing as we went. We'd already descended three thousand feet, according to Tommy, and had over five thousand to go.

Rosina stopped to complain about her blisters every so often, and Toni was hanging close to the wall of the canyon, trying to look very casual about it. Toni is probably the gutsiest person I know, but I think she may be afraid of heights. Not so afraid that she doesn't do completely insane things like jump out of airplanes.

Personally, I can relate. I know how it feels to be afraid of something and not want anyone to know.

The Bright Angel is a beautiful trail, originally formed by an earthquake fault. It crisscrosses Garden Creek most of the way down. And John was right, it was hot in the canyon. Tommy told us the temperature changes by more than twenty degrees from the top to the bottom.

I felt little beads of sweat coursing down my back, and stopped under the shade of a cottonwood tree to take off my sky-blue cotton sweater and tie it around my waist. I held my hair off my neck and took a drink from my water bottle.

"Hey, Susie, why the big hurry?" Tommy asked, magically appearing a few feet behind me.

You! I felt like shouting at him. *I'm trying to get away from you!* I turned to him and frowned. "My name is Susette, not Susie," I snapped.

He smiled that lopsided smile again. "No prob, Susie."

Grrr. I stomped away, careful not to look behind me.

At last we stopped for lunch at Indian Gardens, a place where the path widens into a lush little park dotted with cottonwood trees. We all took out the lunches the hotel had packed for us—ham-and-cheese sandwiches, crackers, apples, brownies. I secretly plucked the slices of ham from my sandwich.

My parents totally disapprove of this, but I don't like eating meat very much. I saw a documentary once about a slaughterhouse, and I've never really enjoyed a hamburger since. It's mostly because I love animals—dogs, cats, cows, pigs, you name it. My grandpa thinks I'm softhearted, and my parents just think I'm nuts.

"Hey, Susie, can I have your ham?"

I jerked around and gave Tommy another of my withering stares. "No. And if you call me Susie one more time, I'm going to punch you in the stomach as hard as I can."

Everybody in the group shut right up. Toni and Allison stared at me as though I had suddenly sprouted a second head. Rosina nearly choked on her cracker. I'm not exactly known for chewing people out.

I stood up, walked to the edge of the trail and stared down at the sparkling river below. I had a feeling of doom settling in my stomach. I was facing the terrifying prospect of getting into that river and, almost as bad, having to spend the next forty-eight hours with Tommy.

There was no way I could escape either one of them.

By the time we'd made it down the Devil's Corkscrew—a series of very tight, very steep switch-backs—and reached the gorgeous suspension bridge that crossed the roaring river at the bottom of the canyon, we were a very silent group.

Debbie wasn't speaking with John because John had just announced that he wasn't going rafting with us the next day. Turns out an old girlfriend of his, named Chrissie or Kristie or Crystal or something like that, was working at Phantom Ranch.

Phantom Ranch, by the way, is a beautiful place at the bottom of the canyon where hikers, rafters, and mule riders can spend the night. In fact, it's where we were staying that night.

Anyway, whatever-her-name-is had the day off tomorrow, John explained, and she had offered to spend it hiking with John up to Ribbon Falls, which John said he'd always wanted to see.

Debbie was obviously furious about this.

"I can't believe you're just ditching your responsibilities," Debbie had whispered to him on our last water stop. "You're going off with your *girlfriend* when you're supposed to be leading this trip. What if something happens to one of the girls?" she'd demanded.

"She's not my girlfriend, Debbie," John had mumbled. "Everything will be fine."

Debbie could talk about responsibility as much as she wanted, but we all knew the real problem. Debbie was jealous. Which I guess is why she made several comments to no one in particular about how wonderful Jim Freeman was, and how much she'd missed him since he'd graduated the year before.

Rosina wasn't talking to Toni, because Toni had put a lizard in her lunchbag. Rosina is a real wuss about anything with scales or more than four legs.

Toni wasn't talking to Allison because Allison had demanded she stop singing Whitney

Houston songs. Toni and Allison may be best friends, but they hate each other's taste in music.

I wasn't talking to Rosina, because I was sick of listening to her complain about how long the hike was and just how badly a person would be mangled if they fell over the edge of the trail. I wasn't talking to Toni, because I was also sick of her Whitney Houston tunes. I wasn't talking to Allison, because Allison had teased me about yelling at Tommy.

And I wasn't talking to Tommy because I hated his guts.

The only good news was that Tommy wasn't talking to me, either.

Three

We all sat around a table in the dining room at Phantom Ranch after dinner that night trying to digest the huge meal we'd just eaten. Jim Freeman, Debbie's friend, had joined us for dinner, and I liked him a lot. He is a year older than Debbie, tall and handsome, with light blond hair, green eyes, and the nicest smile in the world. Debbie kept her back to John and spent most of the meal talking with Jim.

I was feeling almost happy. I loved the ranch, with its rustic wood furniture and Native-American rugs. We had a whole beautiful little cabin to ourselves. They usually reserved private cabins for mule riders, but Mrs. Francis had pulled some strings.

I loved the food, too. Several of the dishes (no meat, I was happy to discover) were based on recipes of the Havasupai Indians. Tommy explained to us that they were a tribe that had lived in the region for hundreds of years. Be-

lieve it or not, Tommy himself was half
Havasupai. I was fascinated by the stories he
told us about his family and his mother's
tribe, although I never would have told him
so.

The Havasupai, like most other Native-
American tribes, I guess, have had a lot of
trouble over the years, and lost almost all of
their land. Without their land they had no
way to support themselves, and their community grew impoverished and angry, he told us.
The cultural differences between the Havasupai and the American settlers made them distrust each other. Distrust grew into prejudice,
and the damage was never really fixed.

As I watched Tommy talk, I couldn't help
thinking that he and I actually had some
things in common. I could tell he struggled
with being from two different cultures, just
the way I and my family had. My family had
come from Japan to California in the 1920s,
and they'd had a lot of trouble fitting in. In
the Second World War, when the United
States was fighting Japan, the distrust of Japa-
nese-Americans got so bad that the American
government put them in camps that were like
prisons—people who hadn't done anything
wrong except be Japanese.

I know a lot about this because my grandpa

and grandma (she died when I was only four) and my dad lived in one of those camps for two years, when my dad was a little kid. When he first told me about that, I felt so sad and angry, I cried. I couldn't believe people as wonderful as my grandpa and his family could be treated so badly. But you know what the amazing thing is? My grandpa isn't mad. He's very proud to be American. He's more patriotic than anyone I've ever met.

I only realized my eyes had settled on Tommy's face when he looked up at me and locked his gaze on mine. For this one weird instant I felt like we knew each other. Like we were so much the same, we could read each other's minds. An instant later I felt like an idiot and stared back down at my cup of tea.

What was I thinking? I hated Tommy. He was totally rude and obnoxious.

"Are you girls excited about your adventure tomorrow?" John asked, leaning back contentedly in his chair. I was happy he filled up the awkward silence.

Debbie gave Jim a smile. "Jim and I are going to have a wonderful time together."

"I can't wait to go river-running," Toni said excitedly. "Are we going to go over any waterfalls or anything?"

Tommy laughed. "I hope not. A waterfall can chew you up pretty bad. We'll have plenty of thrills without a waterfall. Rapids, standing waves, whirlpools."

I started fumbling with my napkin. I realized I was gripping it tightly in my fist. My calmness was evaporating.

"Wow," Allison said. "How big are the rapids?"

"Oh, they'll be plenty big," Tommy said. "The river is running a little low, which makes it rough. You just wait."

I started shredding my crumpled napkin to bits.

"Is it dangerous?" Rosina asked.

Tommy shrugged. "Not if you follow directions. Not if you avoid holes and naked boulders." He chuckled. "Not if you know how to swim."

At this point I must have let out a little squeak, because everyone turned and looked at me.

I saw a look of concern come into Allison's eyes. "Jeez, Susette, are you feeling all right? You're as white as a sheet."

Toni grabbed my hand, releasing hundreds of minuscule pieces of napkin. "Are you okay?" she asked.

I tried to steady my breathing before I answered. "I'm fine," I said, hoping they wouldn't hear the wobble in my voice.

"Debbie is going *nuts,*" Toni announced gleefully from the sink where she was brushing her teeth.

"She practically turned green when Kristie came over to the table," Allison said, giggling. "Didn't you just know Kristie had to be gorgeous?"

"It us isterical," Toni said through a mouthful of toothpaste.

"But she has Jim, who isn't too bad himself," Allison said, pulling her Red Sox nightshirt over her head. "He and Debbie were an item last year, right, Toni? He was the guy who was eating cereal in your kitchen practically every afternoon?"

"Uh-huh," Toni said, rinsing her mouth. She glanced at Allison in the mirror. "He's nice. Definitely cute. And I could use a break from Debbie making goo-goo eyes at John. It makes me sick."

Rosina plumped the goose-down pillow she'd stashed in her backpack. Her suitcases were at the hotel on the rim, of course. "This is turning into a soap opera—Debbie and John, John and Kristie, Debbie and Jim." The goose-down pillow, by the way, is classic Rosina. She has only her backpack to store the necessities of life, and she brings her pillow from home. Toni teases her about this at every opportunity.

I pulled down the covers and climbed into bed. "I feel bad for Debbie," I said. "I wonder if John has any idea why she's acting so weird."

"Because she *is* weird," Toni offered helpfully.

Allison shrugged. "Probably not. Guys are such blockheads."

Allison must have caught my look of surprise, because she started laughing. "Trust me, they are. I have five brothers, I know these things."

I sighed and lay back on my pillow. "I don't understand guys at all," I said philosophically.

I saw Allison and Toni share a look. "Lesson number one," Allison said. "When they tease you and call you names, it means they like you."

Suddenly she and Toni and Rosina were all giggling.

I felt a blush start at my neck and creep all the way up to the roots of my hair.

Thankfully, at that moment Debbie poked her head in the door to our room. "Stop giggling in here and turn off the lights. Right now, okay? We have a big day tomorrow."

"Yes sir," Toni said, hopping into bed next to me.

Debbie waited for Allison and Rosina to get into bed and then snapped off the light.

"Good night, you guys," Allison whispered into the darkness.

"Tomorrow's going to be the best," Toni added.

I turned over and snuggled under the covers, hoping that somehow that would be true.

The air was so heavy, I could hardly breathe. Somewhere off in the distance I heard the low rumble of thunder. Suddenly I realized I was up to my neck in water. I looked around in a panic, my heart pounding in my chest.

It was that lake. Thunder Lake, Camp Tuckahoe, a place I would never forget. I recognized the sandy banks, the thick forest of pine trees, but everything was slightly off, slightly blurry. And the sky was growing black as clouds rushed in to blot out the sun.

My breath was coming in gasps as I flailed my arms and legs, desperate to keep my head above water. Desperate to keep the water from sucking me under. A bolt of lightning tore apart the sky.

"Help!" I screamed, but it came out as a whisper.

I had to reach the bank. I was pinwheeling my arms, trying as hard as I could to propel myself toward the shore.

I don't know how to swim, I thought miserably. *I can't swim.*

I was paddling my arms and legs, choking for my next breath. At last I was getting closer to shore. Another clap of thunder rolled through the sky. *Paddle your arms,* I ordered myself. *Kick your legs.* My limbs were burning with exhaustion, fighting the powerful tug of the water. *Almost there. Almost there,* I kept telling myself.

But when I looked up the shore was hundreds of feet farther away. The water was pulling me down. Pulling. I couldn't fight it anymore.

As another bolt of lightning split the sky, I watched the water close over my head. The water pulled me down farther and farther into its blackness . . .

"Rise and shine!"

I opened one eye. I opened the other eye.

Toni was doing a little dance in the middle of the room.

"Get up, you lazy bums!" she shouted.

Allison chucked a pillow at her.

The bright morning sunlight spilled into the room, and I was suddenly overwhelmed by the memory of the nightmare I'd had. A drowning nightmare, just like the ones I'd been having since I was eight years old. But this one was even more terrifying. More vivid.

I closed my eyes and opened them again. A shiver traveled the length of my body. My eyes wandered from Toni to Allison to Rosina, to the square of yellow sunlight on the floor. I breathed a big sigh of relief.

I was not at camp. I was not in that lake. I was at the bottom of the Grand Canyon, waking up to a beautiful morning in my cabin at Phantom Ranch, surrounded by my three favorite traveling buds.

Nothing bad was going to happen. I just had to believe that.

Rosina was taking so much time in the bathroom putting on a cucumber mask or some dumb thing like that, that I grabbed my toothbrush, toothpaste, soap, and washcloth and headed for the hall. I knew there was another bathroom nearby. I was still preoccupied by my nightmare, which is the only reason I ever allowed myself to walk out there in my nightgown.

I got to the bathroom, put my hand on the doorknob, and suddenly the door flew open, nearly knocking me over. There, standing in the doorway, wearing nothing but boxer shorts and a T-shirt, was Tommy.

I looked at him. He looked at me. I looked at him. He looked at me—slowly this time, taking in the nightgown and the fuzzy pink slippers with the bunny ears, as I turned from light pink to dark purple.

He gave me that lopsided grin. "I like your slippers."

It would be putting it very mildly to say I wanted to die on the spot. I wanted the walls to crumble, the floor to break through. I really did.

Why am I letting him get to me like this? I demanded of myself as I strode away with as much dignity as a person wearing fuzzy bunny slippers possibly could. *Why?*

An annoying little part of my brain way in the back seemed to know. That part was saying it was because I thought he was handsome. It was because he made me nervous when he looked at me like that, because he made me feel something different than I'd ever felt in my whole life.

I did not feel like listening to that part of my brain.

As I told you already, my parents didn't want me to go on this trip. They hadn't wanted me to be in danger, they hadn't wanted me to be in situations I wasn't prepared for, or to have more freedom than they thought I could handle.

And you know what? Maybe, just maybe, they were right.

Four

"Oh my gosh, oh my gosh, oh my gosh," Allison said worriedly, flying into our room a few minutes later and slamming the door behind her.

I looked up from the floor where I was tying the laces of my hiking boots. "What's up?"

Toni giggled. "Jeez, Ally-Cat. And you always yell at *me* about being hyper in the morning."

"We have to talk, all of us," Allison said, pacing the room. "We might have a very serious problem." She banged on the bathroom door. "Yo, Rosina! Get out here."

Rosina peered out the door, frowning. She still had a green mask smeared all over her face.

"Please?" Allison begged.

Rosina rolled her eyes. She came over and plopped down on the foot of the bed. "What?"

"Spill," Toni commanded.

Allison pushed her long thick hair back over her shoulders. "I'm worried Debbie is really falling for Jim."

Toni cocked her head. "So? It's better than watching her flirt with John."

Rosina narrowed her eyes. "Wait a sec. This is your big news? You got me out of the bathroom for this?"

"I'm worried she's falling for Jim, and that she's really, really mad at John—"

"Al, no offense, but we know this," Toni said patiently.

"Listen," Allison continued impatiently. "I went to get an aspirin from Debbie's room a couple of minutes ago and I overheard her talking with Jim. She was saying how wonderful it would be if she could spend the summer with him rafting."

"Debbie's love life is really fascinating and everything," Rosina said, looking bored. "But it's not really our business."

"Rosina, get a clue," Allison said in annoyance. "It is *too* our business. Why do you think Debbie agreed to travel with us this summer?"

"Because she has a massive crush on John?" I offered.

"Yeah, that's part of it," Allison said. "And

do you know what happens if Debbie and John start hating each other and she falls in love with Jim?" She gave us a few seconds to absorb that.

"She won't travel with us anymore?" I said slowly.

"And what happens if she refuses to travel with us?" Allison persisted.

"The best summer of our lives is over practically before it got started," I answered.

"We go home and stay there," Toni said, her face stricken.

"No sailing in Maine," Allison said.

"No New York City," I added.

"No Spain," Rosina said.

Toni groaned. "No Paris or Greece or anyplace."

"I'll have to spend the summer baby-sitting my little sisters," I said miserably.

Allison bit her lip. "I'll have to work in my dad's office."

"I'll have to go to summer school," Toni muttered.

Rosina's eyes lit up. "I'll have to go to camp," she said, not looking very sad at all.

"Rosina!" the rest of us shrieked.

"Just kidding." Rosina shrugged. "I really would hate to miss Spain."

"There's one thing I'm absolutely sure of,"

Toni said determinedly, tapping her foot on the ground.

"What?" I asked.

"We can't let this happen."

"And what are we supposed to do about it?" Rosina demanded.

Toni got that gleam in her eye that always makes me nervous. "I just so happen to have the perfect plan."

"And what would that be?" Allison asked, looking just as suspicious as I felt.

"Simple," Toni said. "We make sure Jim doesn't fall for Debbie."

"And how do we do that?" Rosina wanted to know.

"Debbie's no great catch, if you ask me. She's a bossy know-it-all," Toni said confidently. "Jim will easily find somebody he likes better. We just have to point out to him Debbie's . . . uh . . . less appealing qualities," Toni said.

"What if he doesn't think they're unappealing?" I asked.

Toni shrugged. "Easy. We make up some that are."

"Debbie, you want my cranberry muffin?" Toni asked sweetly. Debbie, Jim, and the four of us were gathered around a big table in the dining room at Phantom Ranch, finishing up our breakfast. Kristie and John had already taken off on their hike up to the waterfall. "You only had three bowls of cereal," Toni continued. "You usually eat much more than that for breakfast."

Debbie shot Toni a puzzled look. "I had two bowls of cereal. And no, I don't want your muffin."

Silence. Allison was shuffling her feet under the table. "So, Debbie, did you take your, uh . . . medication yet?" Allison asked.

Debbie turned and stared at her. "What medication?"

"You know. For your . . . condition."

Debbie shook her head. "No. I have no idea what you're talking about."

"That's okay, Debbie," Toni said quickly. "I understand if you don't want to, um, talk about it . . ." She gave Jim a significant look. ". . . right now."

I just stared down at my bowl of cereal. This was crazy. I submerged the little Cheerios under the milk with the back of my spoon and watched them pop back up. I was way too nervous to eat.

Debbie got up from the table, shaking her head. "You guys are even weirder than normal today. Let's get going before it gets any worse."

"So," Toni said, casually sidling up next to Jim as we headed out of the ranch. "Debbie sure has changed a lot since last year, don't you think?"

Jim looked at her uncertainly. "Uh . . . no. Actually, she seems pretty much the same to me. I mean, she's more grown up and everything."

Toni's face instantly turned grim. "So I guess you haven't heard . . ." Her voice trailed off.

Jim looked immediately concerned. "Heard about what?"

"Her, uh, problem."

"No." Jim looked truly worried. "What problem?"

I could tell Toni was thinking fast. In typical fashion she had waded right into her lie without even figuring out what she was going to say.

"Her . . . um . . . tapeworm," Toni finally finished at the exact same moment that Allison said, "body fungus."

The two of them glanced at each other in momentary panic.

"Tapeworm," Allison said.

"Fungus," Toni said at the same time.

Jim looked completely perplexed.

"She, uh, has this terrible fungus growing all over her body as a result of her tapeworm," Toni clarified.

"It's a very unusual condition," Allison added.

Toni nodded. "Unusual and terrible."

Jim shook his head in bewilderment. "Boy, I had no idea. That sounds awful." He looked at Debbie, who was walking with Rosina several yards ahead of us, his eyes full of compassion. "You'd never know. She looks so healthy."

Toni and Allison both nodded solemnly. "But whatever you do, don't say anything to her about it, okay?" Toni said.

"She's very sensitive," Allison added.

"Sure, I understand," Jim said. He hurried his pace a little to catch up to Debbie. "Tapeworm," he muttered under his breath, wincing.

Toni flashed a smile at Allison. They shared a silent high five.

I quickened my pace, too. I had enough to worry about without my friends acting like complete and total morons.

* * *

I was trying to enjoy the incredible sights, I really was, as we followed the zigzagging trail to a calm part of the river where Tommy was setting up the raft. But watching the river shooting over rocks, speeding by trees, frothing into rapids, made me so nervous I felt numb.

This is fun, I kept saying to myself. *I'm having fun.*

"Sus, you look like you're heading for the gallows," Debbie said, looking over at me. "Are you okay?"

I gave her a determined nod. "Yeah. This is fun."

"You sure?" I could see the concern in Debbie's eyes, and I felt consumed with guilt for the whole tapeworm episode.

"Yeah." It came out as kind of a squeak.

Debbie's face was so nice and so sympathetic that for a second I really wanted to tell her the truth about how I was feeling. Maybe I should have told I was terrified of the water, and that I was dreading this more than I would dread having every single one of my teeth pulled.

But somehow I couldn't. I felt so pathetic. Here I was, the youngest person on the trip, afraid of water. I was scared that if I told them the truth, they would never take me seriously again.

And more than that, I almost hoped that if I didn't tell them how scared I really was, then maybe it wouldn't be true.

"Hey, look! There's the raft!" Toni shouted, racing ahead.

Sure enough, there it was. A big inflatable raft. And there was Tommy smiling and waving at us. Neither of the sights was very comforting to me.

For the next hour we stood on the bank of the rushing river learning about rafting. I tried as hard as I could to listen, to ignore my pounding heart, my sweating palms, all of the feelings from my dream the night before, and the funny looks Jim kept giving Debbie.

We learned about rowing, steering, getting yourself out of a trouble spot. Then we got into the gory details, like what to do if the raft flipped over and how to recognize and avoid whirlpools. "Now, if the raft does flip and you find yourself heading downriver," Jim instructed, "get your feet out in front of you. If you're going to hit a boulder, I'd rather you find it with your feet. Everybody understand?"

Gulp. "Yeah," I said weakly.

Minutes later a life preserver was pulled

over my head, and I found myself wading out into the freezing river. I felt like a zombie. It was the first time I had been in water higher than my knees since I was eight years old.

It didn't feel all that great.

I climbed into the raft and somebody stuck an oar in my hands. Jim untied the raft, and both he and Tommy pushed us clear of the bank. The raft pitched as they both jumped on, and I drew in a sharp breath.

Oh no. Oh no. We're going to flip over right here and now. I'm going to be carried down this river to my watery grave. Somebody DO SOMETHING!

By the time I'd finished my little panic attack, the raft had righted itself and we were heading smoothly down the river.

"We're off!" Tommy shouted.

Five

This is fine. This is easy. No problem. This is great. Isn't this fun? I was so busy talking to myself that I didn't realize that I was clutching my oar with all my might. I looked down and was horrified to discover it wasn't my oar at all, it was Tommy's arm! I snatched it away as fast as I could.

Tommy glanced at me. Was it laughter I saw in his eyes?

"You okay?" he asked.

"Yeah. Totally fine," I snapped. "Perfect. This is great." I gestured to the gorgeous vista in front of us to make my point.

"This is so *awe*some!" Toni shouted up at the sky.

The views really were breathtaking, although that wasn't the reason that *I* couldn't breathe. High on every side were the walls of the canyon, flaming red in the morning sunlight. The river was a brilliant green—the color of jade—and the sky was a perfect blue arc above us.

"Row, Sus! You've got to row!" Tommy shouted at me.

I frowned at him and tried slithering my oar back and forth in the water. That was a good thing, actually. It gave me something to concentrate on besides panicking. Slowly, slowly, I started to breathe again. I started to hear the chatter around me, Toni telling Jim about how she doesn't sleep at night because her sister snores so badly, Allison and Rosina arguing about whose blisters from yesterday's hike were worse. I even laughed when I overheard Toni tell Jim in a hushed voice that Debbie had a poster of Axl Rose over her bed.

I was getting used to the feeling of the river. It was fast and powerful, but not *really* fast. The first few bumps we'd hit made me jump a mile, but after that I started to calm down. The raft was surprisingly stable. I had several more catastrophic fantasies, but the truth was, these weren't bumps that were going to flip us over.

The river twisted and turned in broad loops. Occasionally it was met by creeks flowing down the ravines of the canyon's walls. The colors and stripes in the walls changed as we went. Tommy said the walls could practically teach you the history of the world, every layer showing a different part of the world's history.

For the next few minutes the river turned totally serene and quiet. We pulled up our oars and leaned back in the sun, letting the gentle water carry us along exactly where it wanted to.

"Anybody hungry?" Jim asked, looking a little nervously at Debbie.

"Absolutely, totally starving," Debbie said. "I could practically eat this raft. I don't know what's gotten into me."

I saw Allison clamp her hand over her mouth.

Jim nodded nervously. "Okay, time to pull over and eat lunch. This is a nice, calm little backwater here to tie up the raft."

I felt my heart soar. I almost shouted in pure joy. We were stopping for lunch! Our trip was half over!

We rowed to the side of the river and hopped out one at a time. I almost kissed the ground when I reached the bank.

I had to smile as I took off my life preserver and shook out my stiff legs. *This really isn't so bad,* I told myself happily. Clearly Tommy had been exaggerating when he'd talked about how rough the river sometimes got. Because today it was calm. Today was my lucky day.

For the first time, I felt like everything really might be okay.

Finding a place to eat lunch on the side of the river is not as easy as you might think. Rising up on every side, as I've explained, are high, steep cliffs and mesas. So the plan was, we'd climb the side of one of the shorter mesas, and eat lunch on top.

You can't just climb up, either. You need ropes, so that if you fall you don't break your neck. Part of this adventure, Jim explained, was to give us an introductory course in technical rock climbing. This actually looked pretty scary. I mean, we're talking at least forty feet straight up with very little to hold on to. I saw Rosina swallow hard, and even Allison looked dubious. Toni, of course, was ready to rock and roll. And to tell you the truth, I wasn't very scared either. I was so overjoyed to be on dry land, we could be crawling across the Mojave desert for all I cared.

Jim started pulling equipment out of his backpack and passing it out.

"Wait one second. I am not putting this on

my head," Rosina said when Jim handed her a helmet.

The helmets were pretty geeky-looking—bright yellow with a strap that went under your chin.

"Rosina, you have to," Jim insisted. "I really don't want you smashing your head against a rock."

Debbie gave her one of those patented older-sister looks. "Let's not argue about this."

Rosina sullenly stuck it on her head.

"I'm glad we're wearing helmets," Toni whispered to me.

I nodded, figuring she liked the idea of keeping her head in one piece.

"Debbie has the kind of hair that just can't take hat head," she finished.

I couldn't help giggling.

Next Jim passed out climbing harnesses. A harness is a long thick strap that wraps tightly around the tops of your legs and your waist. Toni is so little, hers wrapped around about eight times. Rosina was annoyed, because hers kept getting bunched up in her shorts.

Anyway, you tie a rope to your harness, and the person at the top of the rock pulls up the rope bit by bit so there's never too much slack.

So the next question is, how do you get a

person and a rope up to the top of the cliff in the first place? Well, you get an expert like Jim, who goes up first, sticking a series of metal peglike things with the rope threaded through into crevices in the rock. When he gets past one peg, he drives another into the rock, so that the rope is always secure several feet above him in case he falls. Once he gets all the way to the top, he ties the rope to a big boulder and throws the other end down to secure the next climber.

Debbie climbed up right after him, pulling out the pegs as she went. She is very agile and seemed to find little holes and ledges in the rock face easily. At one point she stumbled a little, and the rope caught her. "Whoa!" she cried, and we all gasped.

When she reached the top, Jim gave her a hand up over the lip of the cliff, untied her, and threw the rope down for the next person.

I could see Toni watching them like a hawk for any sign of romance.

I was up next. I threaded the rope through my harness and tied it the way Jim had shown us. As I felt the rope in my hands, I was a little surprised by how old it seemed. But it looked strong. It had to be. Tommy checked everything to make sure I'd done it right.

"On rope!" I cried, looking up into the

sun. That's what Jim told us you're supposed to say.

Tommy pointed out the first good foothold, and I hoisted myself up the rock.

"Go, baby!" Toni yelled.

"You look great!" Allison yelled.

Rock climbing is harder than you might think. It's tiring on your arms and legs. You have to trust all your weight to some tiny little groove in the rock that's only about an inch or two wide. You're thinking, *there is absolutely no way can this thing hold me,* but then it does. I scrambled to the top pretty quickly, and everyone cheered.

"Susie, you're the best!"

I didn't need to look down to know who'd shouted that. I smiled a little in spite of myself.

Jim helped me detach myself from the rope, and we threw it back down for Rosina, who came next.

Everybody did pretty well. Rosina was scared and slow, and she got all bent out of shape when she scraped her shin on the rock.

Allison blazed her own path, but she got too far over to one side of the rock and couldn't find a good foothold.

"What am I supposed to do now?" she asked, looking up at us.

"That's what you get for being such a hot-shot, Ally-Cat," Toni shouted up at her.

I could tell she was getting tired, because her legs were starting to shake the way they do when you hold one position too long.

"You have to creep back over till you find a hold," Jim shouted.

Allison tugged on the rope tied to her harness. "Can't you just pull me up?" she asked.

Jim laughed and shook his head.

At last she found the path the rest of us had taken, and made her way up.

Toni came next. She spent several minutes looking for a foothold to start on, but couldn't seem to find one.

"Just get a boost, would you?" Allison called to her. "We're going to be here all day." As I said before, she and Toni read each other's minds.

Toni resentfully accepted a boost from Tommy. But she was mad about it, which is why she came up way too fast. We all gasped as she lost her footing and fell. The rope caught her and she dangled there for a while, laughing, as Debbie turned a pasty shade of white.

Tommy, of course, came up effortlessly.

Once we were all safely at the top, we took

our lunches and water bottles out of our back-packs.

"Don't ever do that!" Jim suddenly thundered at Rosina out of the blue.

We were all shocked. Jim isn't the kind of guy you'd expect to have a temper.

Poor Rosina looked like she was going to jump out of her skin. "Do what?" she asked timidly.

Jim pointed to the rope under her hiking boot. "Never walk on a rope you use to climb. *Never.*" He held up the rope. "Everybody hear that? If you step on the rope, it grinds dirt and rocks and other debris into the fibres. Over time it will make the rope dangerously weak. Got it?"

We all nodded mutely.

"Kind of a tyrant, isn't he?" Allison whispered to Debbie. Debbie just ignored her.

So for the rest of our lunch, we were careful to step around the rope.

Not surprisingly, Allison and Toni spent the entire time hammering away at Debbie. And it really got out of hand when Debbie went off to go to the bathroom. (There were about three bushes on our little plateau. We all just sort of looked the other way. You get used to that kind of thing pretty fast.)

"We're all crossing our fingers that Debbie

will get into, uh . . . Dudley Community College," Toni said in a hushed voice, picking at the crumbs of her brownie. "It's a longshot, but we can hope, can't we?"

"*Dudley* Community College. I've never heard of it. Where is that?" Jim asked.

Awkward pause.

"Off Randall Road," Toni said at exactly the moment Allison said, "near Jones Bridge."

They turned to one another in alarm.

"Behind the 7-Eleven," Allison said, just as Toni said, "across from King Food."

"It's hard to describe," Toni said quickly.

"I know I always get lost when I go there," Allison offered.

Jim looked thoroughly confused. "Why would Debbie go there? She told me she's going to Berkeley."

"Well . . . uh . . . it's hard to be honest all the time," Toni said.

No joke, I thought, looking ashamedly at my half-eaten peanut-butter sandwich.

"And with her grades and all . . ." Toni gave Jim a significant look.

"What are you talking about? Debbie's a great student," Jim protested.

Toni just nodded at him in a meaningful way. "Well, maybe you don't know Debbie as well as you thought you did."

Jim shrugged. "Maybe you're right." He looked a little impatient. "Listen, I'm going to unpack the equipment we'll need for the repel down the cliff. Why don't you all finish up your lunch and then we'll have a quick seminar on repelling." He walked away, shaking his head.

"Dudley Community College?" Allison demanded as soon as he was out of earshot. "What was that about?"

Toni looked slightly embarrassed. "Sorry, it just popped into my head." She frowned. "And why did you have to mess up my story with the 7-Eleven and all that?"

Allison frowned back. "I was trying to help. You could at least figure out a reasonable lie before you get started."

"Like you could do better," Toni snapped.

"I couldn't do worse," Allison snapped back.

"Fine," Toni said. She stomped away in a huff.

Right over our rope.

"Don't you think Debbie should go first?" Toni whispered innocently to Jim as we prepared to go back down the cliff to the river. "She's such a klutz, and this way we can all help her."

Jim shook his head a little distractedly. "Let's go in the order I arranged. Debbie will be fine."

We had just finished our fifteen-minute seminar on the art of repelling and were getting ready to go. Repelling is even more complicated than climbing up the rock. It basically means leaning your weight back on a rope and walking down at a ninety-degree angle to the cliff. It requires more equipment, too. For instance, you have this clasplike thing called a carabeener. Isn't that a great word? Toni went around saying "Carabeeeener," for the next ten minutes, until Debbie told her to shut up.

You clamp the carabeener into your harness, then clamp a metal thing called a figure eight—shaped like, surprise, a figure eight—to your carabeener. You then thread the climbing rope through the figure eight. It sounds very complicated to describe, but it actually not so difficult. Just *make sure,* if you ever go rock climbing, you have somebody who really knows what they're doing show you how to do everything.

We put our helmets back on and we were ready to roll. (Or walk, hopefully.) Tommy went first, and made it look easy. I went next and made it look hard.

I'll tell you, it doesn't feel very natural. You're all hitched up to this rope, and you have to trust it completely, because gravity would send you straight to the bottom of the canyon.

The hardest part is the first step off the cliff. You have to lean back, putting all of your weight into the rope. My own personal preference is to stay vertical—you know, head over feet—but that doesn't work here. So I started to lean and take a few tiny steps backward over the edge of the cliff, praying the rope would hold me. I looked back over my shoulder, at the river below. It looked like a very long way down. My stomach sort of seized up. But then I reminded myself, at least this was dry land. So what if the ground was at completely the wrong angle? It was better than water.

Everybody was cheering as I disappeared over the lip of the cliff.

"Lean back! Trust the rope!" Jim was shouting at me. "If you try to stay vertical, your feet will slip out from under you."

I let a little more rope, so that I was almost sitting, my legs sticking out in front of me, guiding me lightly over the rock face. I kept them wide apart for balance so I would swing into the rock.

"You're doing great!" Tommy called from below.

My hand felt raw from gripping the rope too tightly. *Relax,* I kept telling myself. *You can do this.*

I loosened my grip and let the rope slide through the figure eight a little more quickly, shuffling my feet to catch up. I took one bounce over a jutting rock that made the rope groan. For a moment it took my breath away.

"I think the rope is straining!" I yelled up into the bright sun.

"It's fine! You're doing great!" Debbie shouted back.

I looked back over my shoulder again. I couldn't believe how far I had come. I was only about ten feet from the ground. Carefully, triumphantly, I made it to level ground, unthreaded the rope, and looked up at all the faces nervously peering down at me from above.

"Off rope!" I shouted, and they all started applauding. Tommy clapped me on the back.

Jim pulled the rope up, and got Rosina ready for her repel.

It took half an hour to get Rosina to take that first step backward off the cliff. She was panicked.

"The rope won't hold me. I know it won't,"

she kept wailing. I personally felt very sympathetic to her right then. Everybody coaxed and cajoled from the top, and Tommy and I shouted encouragement from the bottom. When she finally took the step, we all screamed and cheered.

Toni, as you might guess, literally bounced down the wall. She took these giant swinging steps, pushing herself off from the wall and swinging back so hard we were all terrified she was going to flatten her face. Debbie screamed at her a few times, but I could tell Toni was having too much fun to stop.

Allison was a pro. She was careful, but quick. We cheered when she got to the bottom, and she smiled her cool Allison smile. "No big deal," she murmured.

I was in a great mood when Debbie was gearing up to go. The sun was bright and the sky was a perfect blue over our heads. Repelling for me was a triumphant feeling of fear rather than a queasy feeling of fear, the way a certain other thing which I won't mention is.

I sat in my bright yellow maillot bathing suit and hiking shorts leaned against a rock, my face tipped up toward the sun, watching Debbie, a cutout against the bright sky, stepping nervously out over the cliff.

I watched as she leaned way back, gripping the rope in her hand, letting out more and more until she was hanging far out over the precipice. She took two more steps down when I heard the most frightening noise. A sickening straining and ripping sound tore through the air of the silent canyon.

Debbie's scream was echoed by Toni's, mine, Rosina's, Allison's, Jim's, and Tommy's as we watched the rope split in her hands and send her hurtling downward.

Six

It felt as though it happened in slow motion. Our screams were suspended through the canyon as Jim reached down in one lightning-fast motion and grabbed Debbie's outstretched hand. He stopped her fall in midair. We all gasped again as he strained to hold her and keep his balance without tumbling over the edge.

"Ohmygod, ohmygod," Toni was crying, her fingernails digging into my leg.

Jim's struggle to keep his balance over the steep, craggy edge seemed to last forever, but finally he hoisted Debbie up to safety. We all collapsed in relief. Toni started crying and Allison put her arms around her.

"I'm okay," Debbie yelled to us in a trembling voice. "I'm really okay." She lay back on the rock, way above, her body still shaking with strain and fear.

I hugged Toni, Allison hugged me, I hugged Rosina. For one insane instant I even thought of hugging Tommy, which I didn't actually do.

We were all so overwhelmed by happiness and relief that we forgot one little tiny problem. Debbie and Jim were stranded on a canyon wall, and the five of us needed to find our way out and get them help.

Tommy studied the river with a serious look on his face. I could tell Debbie's near fall had shaken him just as much as it had the rest of us. "The river is running rough up ahead, but we'd better get going if we're going to get Debbie and Jim out of here before dark."

I looked nervously at the water. Thankfully it still looked pretty calm to me. "We're just going to take the raft ourselves?" I asked, wishing my voice didn't sound so squeaky.

Tommy shrugged. "We don't have much choice." He must have seen the stricken look on my face, because he smiled a little. "Don't worry, Sus. I've taken a hundred rafts down this river."

Allison started packing up her backpack. "Where are we going exactly?"

"To the bottom of Hermit's Trail, where we can hike back up to the south rim and find help," Tommy explained, handing out life jackets.

"Let's go, let's go," Toni said, climbing into the raft. "I don't want to give those lovebirds too much time together." A worried look crossed her face. "I wonder if the tapeworm thing will come up?"

We all started laughing, relieved to be letting off a little steam.

But Tommy's face was still serious. "Hey, you guys, before we go, I just want to warn you." He squinted into the sunlight. "See that?" He pointed to a bend in the river up ahead.

"See what?" Toni asked.

"The rock formation that juts out into the river up there."

"Yeah," I said, seeing clearly now a swirling patch of water.

"That's a whirlpool. They are deadly. A whirlpool like that will drag you down in seconds, pop you up, and pull you back down again. Your life jacket won't save you. It's more powerful than you can believe." He looked at each of us. "We'll be heading over Salt Creek Rapids and Granite Rapids, and the river's running low. It's going to be rough. If the raft goes over, try to recognize the whirlpools so you can avoid them."

"If the raft goes over?" Rosina asked worriedly.

"Yeah. I'll do my best to keep us up, but just in case."

My heart had started its heavy thud. I opened my mouth but no sound came out.

I listened numbly as Tommy gave us a last crash course in steering the raft and we piled in.

But everything has been fine so far, I comforted myself. I had already spent two hours in that raft on the river and everything had been fine. The river couldn't change that much, could it?

It could. The river turned from silent and peaceful to fast and frothy within a few hundred yards. My breath was coming in shallow gasps as the raft flew over the rapids.

"Yahooooo!" Toni shouted, her voice echoing around the walls of the canyon.

"Waaaaaaa!" Rosina screamed, laughing as we hit a bump.

They all seemed to find the speed thrilling. I was terrified. I was gripping my oar with all my might, trying to concentrate on paddling just the way Jim and Tommy had taught us. I didn't want to look ahead, I didn't want to look behind, I just wanted to paddle to Hermit's Trail and get out of this raft as fast as I could.

"Hold on tight!" Tommy shouted, his voice quickly lost in the roar of the river. "Salt Creek Rapids, here we come!"

Wait a minute! We weren't even at the rapids yet? What was I going to do? I couldn't hold on any tighter if I were surgically attached to the raft.

We came round a bend and the water turned savage. I mean it. One second it was rough and the next second it was wild. The raft suddenly felt tiny and frail amidst the enormous craggy rocks.

I screamed as we hit a boulder. We ricocheted off it into another even bigger one. I screamed again.

"It's okay, Sus!" Tommy shouted at me. "The raft'll stay up."

Although Toni still looked overjoyed by the speed of the ride, Rosina and Allison were getting scared, too.

Though I was afraid my heart might explode, I knew that however scared I was, as long as the raft stayed up, I'd make it. I'd be okay.

And if the raft didn't stay up . . . well, I couldn't even think about that. I couldn't think of how I'd survive in rushing, surging water with no idea how to swim.

Please stay up, I prayed silently. *Please.*

It was as though somebody up there heard my prayer, because suddenly we turned a bend and the river widened and calmed. The roar of the rapids quieted to a gentle rushing noise. I took a deep breath and tried my best to unkink my tense, knotted muscles.

Suddenly the canyon seemed beautiful to me again. It was peaceful in the pink afternoon light. I tried to peel my fingers from my oar, lean back and relax a little in the warm sun. I spotted an eagle at the top of a butte.

Suddenly I saw Tommy tense. I sat up too, instantly alert. "Heads up!" he shouted.

I looked up. There were no rapids. There were no rocks. There were no whirlpools.

There was nothing. The water dropped off into nothing, and we were heading straight for it.

"Hold on!" Tommy shouted. I could hear the fear in his voice, and it sent ice through my veins.

There was no way to turn back. The river

hurled us closer and closer. At the final moment before flying over the precipice into the roaring waterfall, I closed my eyes and held on for dear life.

Seven

One moment we were flying through the air and the next we were tumbling into foaming, angry water.

I don't think I opened my eyes. When I felt the ice-cold water surround my limbs and cover my head, I knew what had happened. The raft had flipped. I struggled under the dark surging water to turn my body right side up. To figure which side that was.

When at last my head broke the surface, I felt my lungs would explode. I gasped for breath as waves and rapids fought to take me under again. A million strange thoughts were rushing around my head. Thoughts that came in little bursts with no beginning and no end. It was a feeling of pure terror I'd had once before and hoped I'd never, ever have again.

I didn't know where anyone else was. I was too panicked to look. I paddled my arms and legs furiously, desperate to keep my head above water, desperate just to keep breathing. The water was so cold it made me almost delirious. I think I would have frozen to death if the adrenaline hadn't been pumping through my body.

As I careened toward a boulder, I suddenly remembered in some broken way about keeping your legs in front of you. I struggled against the river to get them out there.

Wham! My feet smacked against the boulder. If it had been my head, I would not have lived to tell you this story.

But I was able to push off so hard I actually propelled myself into a calmer stretch of the river. Suddenly the roar let up and at last I could hear my own weird, disconnected thoughts.

Then, magically, I focused on the most wonderful sight in the whole world. The shore! It was right there, just fifteen or twenty feet away. Even with my nonexistent swimming abilities, I could manage that at least.

I was paddling and flailing as fast as I could. I could practically feel the bank, it was practically in my grasp, when a current took hold of me. It was gentle at first. It was pulling me along the shore, so I didn't try to fight it.

But then it got stronger and faster. I realized in a panic that it wasn't going to deposit me on the shore. It was pulling me away, and I couldn't get out of its hold.

I wrestled against it, but it just got stronger.

In one frightening moment of deadly clarity I realized where it was taking me. The whirling circle of water was sickeningly familiar. It was a whirlpool.

My feet were sucked into its grip first. Then my head. I was totally submerged when it flung me back to the surface. I took a deep, ragged breath before I was sucked under again. Deeper and deeper into the darkness.

And then everything went black.

I heard a shout. Then I felt a strong arm around my waist. I was torn from the steely clutch of the whirlpool and felt the impact of a rock. I can't tell you exactly what happened, but I know that a few seconds later I was lying on the bank coughing and choking and gasping for air.

When I fully came to, Tommy was kneeling beside me, holding my head in his lap. His expression was full of worry.

I wanted to thank him, to tell him I was

okay, but I couldn't find any words. I just blinked and held my hand to my throat.

"God, Sus, are you okay?"

I nodded mutely.

"You really scared me, you know that?"

I nodded again. "Th-thank you," I managed in a raspy whisper.

"What did you say?"

"Thank you," I whispered again.

He shook his head and smiled. "I couldn't exactly let you drown, could I?"

I just shrugged.

He ruffled my wet hair and laughed. "Can you sit up?"

I struggled to a sitting position. "Where are the others?" I asked, suddenly consumed by worry as I remembered what had happened. The last few seconds before we plummeted into the waterfall came back to me; my friends' faces as pale and streaked with fear as my own.

"They're okay. The river carried them down a few hundred feet and they made it to shore with the raft," he explained. "I saw them get that far, then swam to the opposite bank and ran up the shore to find you."

I nodded again, unsure of what to say.

He held his right hand with his left and cradled it against his chest. "The only problem is, spinning out of that whirlpool, you and I crashed into a rock pretty hard." He smiled ruefully. "I took most of the blow and cracked my wrist."

My eyes widened in alarm. "Oh no. Let me look."

He looked down at his hand and gingerly tried to hold it out. I knew he was in a lot of pain.

I gently held his hand in both of mine. I could tell by the unnatural angle of his wrist and the way it had already swelled that it was probably broken. "Hurts, doesn't it?" I asked.

He shrugged a little. "Kinda."

I had dealt with enough injuries and broken bones in my life, with my two spastic sisters and four little cousins, that I had a pretty good idea of what to do.

"Could you take off your T-shirt?" I asked.

Poor Tommy looked like he was going to fall over when I asked him that. "Um. Okay." He blushed.

"Here. I'll help you," I offered, guiding it around his injured wrist and over his head.

He watched in bafflement as I took his T-shirt to the river and soaked it for a few seconds. I carefully wrapped the cold cloth once around his hand and wrist then tied it around his chest to keep the wrist stable.

"It's like a splint," I said. "It will immobilize your wrist till a doctor can take a look at it. Hopefully the cold water will keep it from swelling too much more."

He nodded and looked down at his make-shift splint. "You're as smart as I thought you were."

I blushed, too, and we sat there in awkward silence for what felt like years.

"S-so now what?" I stammered at last.

"We get back into the water and swim downstream to the raft," Tommy said simply.

That was when it dawned on me. I was supposed to get back in that water. After an experience so terrifying it had almost made my heart stop, he actually expected me to get back in the river and go through it again. Well, I had one answer for that.

"No," I said out loud.

"What do you mean, no?" Tommy asked me.

"I can't do it. I can't go back in that river."

His eyebrows lifted in concern. "Sus, we have no choice. How else are we going to get out of here?"

"Hike?" I suggested weakly.

Tommy looked up at the tall walls of the canyon narrowly imprisoning us and the river. My eyes followed his. High, steep cliffs as far as the eye could see.

"We can't," he said. "Around the next bend the river runs through a gorge and the walls are even narrower than they are here. There's not even a riverbank. The cliffs run straight up from the water's edge."

I shook my head. Was this supposed to be comforting? "No," I said again. "You can go. I'll stay here."

His eyes were pleading now. "You can't stay here. Besides, I need you to help me swim. My right arm is worthless. I can't do it without you."

Suddenly I felt my eyes fill up with warm tears. I demanded them not to spill over, but they didn't pay any attention to me. Big, fat tears rolled relentlessly down my cheeks.

Tommy put his good arm around my shoulders. "It'll be okay, I promise," he said softly. "Please don't cry. We'll just swim a few yards and everything will be fine."

That just made the tears come faster. "I can't," I whispered. "I just can't."

His face was a mixture of sympathy and bafflement. "Why can't you?"

I didn't mean to tell him. I certainly didn't

want to tell him. But the words escaped the same way the tears had. "I'm scared," I said into his shoulder. "I'm so scared."

My grandpa says fear can change everything, and I guess that must be true, because somehow, on the bank of that evil river, I found myself telling a secret I'd never wanted to tell anyone to this obnoxious, extremely cute fifteen-year-old guy. A guy I never thought I'd tell more than my name to.

I'm scared of guys, I reminded myself as I spilled my guts to him. *I never talk to them.*

I told him about Thunder Lake when I was eight, and about all of the terrible nightmares. How I'd never gone in the water after that, never learned to swim.

I told him how scared I was of this rafting trip. How I'd been dreading it every waking second, and even sleeping ones.

And now this. The frightening power of the current and my inability to fight it. The cold blackness of the water, just like before, and the icy fear that I was going to die.

Tommy listened quietly, then held me close while I cried some more.

When I finally came up for air, he was looking at me with an expression I couldn't read.

That's when my heart sank. The expression

was pity. Tommy thought I was the weakest, most pitiful person he'd ever met. And the sad thing was, he was right.

I was.

There was a very, very good reason I had never told anyone this secret before.

It felt like all my weakness and fear and terribleness was just lying out there in the cold open air. I wanted more than anything to pull it all back into myself where it had been hanging around all those years. But I couldn't. It was out there in the open, waiting to mock me.

That was when Tommy said something that surprised me so much I was sure I hadn't heard him right. So I made him say it again.

"You are the bravest person I know."

That's what he said. I swear. I just stared at him in disbelief. "How can you say that?" I demanded in a weepy whisper.

He smiled at me. "There's nothing brave about doing things that don't scare you. The bravest person does the thing that scares her the most." He held me away, looking at me steadily. "Don't you see what I mean? There's no bravery without fear."

There's no bravery without fear. I let that thought roll around in my head for a while. It was a completely new way of looking at it.

Tommy squeezed my shoulders. "Looking your fear in the face is what this adventure is all about, isn't it?"

I put my arm around him and squeezed back, knowing that in some kind of way he was right.

And that I really was going to have to get back into that horrible river.

I was shivering as I ran around collecting sticks. It was equal parts fear, excitement, and hypothermia.

No, that's a lie. It was at least ninety percent fear.

But I was a little excited by this brainstorm I had just had. I couldn't handle the thought of flinging myself at the mercy of the river. I already knew it had none. So I was making us a raft. Tommy thought I was crazy, but then again, he'd known I was crazy for the last hour and the world hadn't exploded or anything.

When I had a nice little pile of sticks and logs, I lined them up and started weaving them together with the long strands of my climbing harness, which had safely landed here with me in my backpack.

After I made lots of tight little knots to se-

cure each of the logs, the raft was ready for
its maiden voyage. It was a little more flexible
than your ideal bunched-together-pile-of-cot-
tonwood-sticks raft, but it was actually kind of
impressive if you didn't study it too closely.

Tommy had been watching me with a
doubtful look on his face, but as I floated it
around the quiet little backwater, he came
over to check it out.

"Wow," he said. "That's really amazing."

I shrugged modestly. "Panic is the mother
of invention."

With my raft ready and our stuff gathered,
there was no other excuse to delay the inevitable. Besides, it was getting dark. The river
was so vicious in the bright sunlight, I shud-
dered even to think of it in darkness.

My hands were shaking so hard I could
hardly fasten my beat-up life preserver together or retie Tommy's splint.

We said good-bye to our little part of the
shore and started wading into the water. Actually, Tommy started wading. I commanded
my legs to, but they just wouldn't. My whole
self mutinied.

Tommy came back and took my hand with
his one good one. "You can do it. I promise."

"M-m-maybe," I said, shaking hard.

I took one tiny step into the river. Two. Tommy squeezed my hand. Three steps. Four. I laid my little homemade raft out in front of us.

Just a few more steps into the roaring rush that would steal us from the safety of this place, that would take all of our decisions away from us.

Another step. I hesitated as the river grew louder and angrier. I was terrified. My heart was like a sledgehammer in my chest. I was shaking uncontrollably.

Here were my fears. I was staring them in the face. Only it felt more like they were staring at me.

"Y-you know what?" I said to Tommy.

"What?" he said.

"I'm v-v-very brave."

Eight

Tommy and I counted to three, I held my breath, and we dove onto our little raft, riding it like a surfboard. The river took hold of us and sent us flying downstream. I was holding Tommy, Tommy was holding me, and we were both holding the raft. Miraculously, we all stayed upright and afloat.

"Granite Rapids, coming up," Tommy said as we raced around a bend. The canyon walls closed in on us, and the ride went from fast to faster. Then we hit the rapids.

Wham! Bam, bam! We were smacking from one rapid to the next. The only thing louder than the boiling water was the crashing of my heart.

I froze when I saw a dark blotch looming before us. A massive naked boulder sticking straight up out of the water, creating a chaos of thundering water around it.

I screamed.

Tommy thought quickly. He maneuvered our

raft so we were flying toward the rock feet first. As we careened into the rock, he pushed off as hard as he could, hurtling us into another rushing current. But at least it was away from the rock.

The gorge opened and we went flying around another bend.

That was when I saw a beautiful sight. Toni, Allison, and Rosina. Tiny little figures screaming to us from the shore. And there was our raft.

I started paddling furiously. Tommy, too—at least as well as he could with one arm. I could see my friends more clearly now. They were wet and bedraggled, but smiling and shouting to us.

"Come *on!*" Toni's voice rose over the roar of the rapids. "You can do it!"

"You're almost here!" Allison screamed.

"Swim!" Rosina ordered.

My heart was pounding and my breath was coming in ragged gasps. We were almost there! Just a little farther! I kept telling myself.

Closer and closer. I could make out their excited faces. They were cheering, jumping up and down. Almost there, almost there.

Now we were less than twenty feet away.

Every cell of my body was focused on touching that shore.

Which is why I didn't notice right away that we were being pulled into a current. Or that just beyond our beloved patch of shore was a field of naked boulders that was turning the water savage.

One second we were headed for land and the next we were being yanked away from it. I saw my friends' faces fall, fear replace excitement.

"Oh noooooo!" I wailed. I paddled as fast and hard as I could. I was stronger than that water. I had to be.

But I wasn't. The water carried us away as though we were no more than a speck of lint, laughing at us for even trying to fight it. We were getting closer, yet were being pulled farther toward the center of the river.

In an instant it became terrifyingly clear. We were going to be carried right past them. We were so close, yet we weren't going to make it. A hundred catastrophic endings flashed through my brain. Images of Tommy and I and our little raft chewed up to bits by the rocks and sent down the river for eternity, our limp dead bodies thrown through falls and rapids, pummeled by rocks.

I was paddling savagely, the adrenaline

pumping through my body. I probably could have lifted a truck at that moment, but I couldn't change the mind of the river.

Ten feet and we were past them. This was it.

Suddenly Toni dove into the water. Another spasm of fear tore at my heart. "Toni, nooooo!" I screamed.

Allison dove in, and Rosina after her. What were they doing? Why did we all have to die? I heard myself sobbing.

Tommy's eyes were wide open. "Come on, come on, come on," I heard him whispering. His arm was clamped around me, rigid with fear.

Toni was actually swimming to us, thrashing the water with all her might. Why wasn't she being hurled downstream the way we were? What was she holding on to?

And then I saw Allison and realized. They had formed a chain! Rosina was holding onto something at the edge of the river, Allison was holding her, and she was holding Toni.

Toni got to within two feet of us and held out her hand. It was so close! I held my hand out, shaking. We were just inches apart, about to fly past. Tommy gave a monstrous kick with his legs, and my hand grasped Toni's.

I held onto her slippery little hand as hard as I could, so hard I probably broke every one of her knuckles, but she didn't flinch. She held my hand tight and pulled. Allison pulled, Rosina pulled. Tommy kicked.

In a last mighty effort, all five of us heaving, we yanked ourselves out of that cruel current, into calmer water, and, at last, onto shore.

We had beaten it. We had beaten the river. It had taken five of us, but we'd done it.

Five wet, dirty, gasping, trembling figures staggered up onto the muddy bank. At last on safe, somewhat dry land, we started screaming.

We shrieked, we yelled, we laughed, we danced around like absolute morons.

We hugged each other. Five of us in a big, dirty group hug. We pulled apart and I hugged Toni.

"Thanks," I said in her ear.

I hugged Allison and Rosina and thanked them, too.

And then I was face to face with Tommy again. This looked sort of familiar. I didn't hesitate this time. I threw my arms around him and he put his one good arm around me. We stayed like that for a long time.

I felt a chill flutter down the length of my body, equal parts fear, exhaustion, relief.

No, that's a lie. It was at least ten percent . . . something else.

"So, you think Jim and Debbie are engaged yet?" Toni asked.

I laughed and leaned comfortably against the side of the raft, soaking up the very last rays of the day's sun.

"Engaged?" Allison demanded in mock disbelief. "Engaged and married. Probably three kids by now."

"Two dogs," Rosina put in.

"A house in the country," I said.

"A grandchild on the way," Toni added.

We all groaned simultaneously.

Half an hour before, we had carried the raft, our tired bodies, and all of our belongings along the narrow patch of shore, past the rocks and swirling angry water. Excuse me, *portaged*. Tommy insisted we not only carried, but portaged, our junk.

We flattened ourselves against a cliff, teetered around a skinny bend, and came upon a stretch of river so calm and slow and happy, you'd think it was your best friend.

We knew better. But we put our raft in and climbed on anyway. Even I agreed it would be better than *portaging* at the moment. And Tommy promised the river would stay wide and calm until the bottom of Hermit's Trail.

So now we were lazily floating downstream, slow but happy.

Tommy's hand was still snug against his chest. The swelling had gone down a little bit. He was streaked with mud, just like the rest of us, but drying off a little. He smiled at me and I smiled back.

I sighed contentedly, looking up at the enormous orange sun dropping down into the canyon. I took a deep breath of warm, pine-scented air.

Here I was, bobbing on the river and actually feeling okay. More than that. I was feeling happy. I felt like I had struggled with the river, struggled with my fears, and beaten them both. And now I didn't feel scared.

Throw me in another field of rapids and I might change my tune, but at that very moment, watching the late-afternoon orangey sunlight set the walls of the canyon on fire,

turning the flat placid river a flaming copper,
I felt I had scored a victory.

And I really did feel brave.

Nine

"Where's Toni?" Rosina asked.

We had reached the bottom of the trail, dragged the raft out of the water, and were deflating it to carry up the long, steep climb.

Our good moods had dissolved into a heavy silence. Getting through the river was euphoric, but we realized we couldn't rest yet. As late as it was, and as tired as we all were, we still had a long difficult trail to navigate.

Going down was rough, but going up was going to be a whole different thing. And Hermit's Trail was considered much more difficult than the Bright Angel.

Worse than that, it was getting cold, and poor Debbie and Jim were still stranded on the top of the mesa, waiting for help. We not only had to climb six thousand feet straight up, but we had to do it fast.

I looked around for Toni. I didn't see her anywhere. "I don't know where she went," I said.

"Leave it to Toni," Allison said in a cranky voice. "Time to pack up this stupid raft and she takes off."

Rosina grunted in agreement.

"Where could she have gone?" I asked.

"I'll try to find her," Tommy said, hopping up to his feet.

Allison waved her arm. "Oh, no you don't. You have to show us how to finish this thing. Toni will be fine. You watch, she'll be back as soon as we're done."

We went back to work on the raft.

"I'm never going to make it to the top," Rosina said grumpily, breaking several minutes of silence.

"Yes, you are," Allison countered.

"No, I'm not," Rosina shot back. "I'm cold, I'm tired, my boots are giving me horrible blisters," she whined. "I'm not going."

"Yes, you are," Allison insisted stubbornly.

"No, I'm not."

"Are so."

"Am not."

"Are so."

I couldn't believe this. My wonderful friends. My heroic saviors, acting like two-year-olds.

"Shut up!" I exploded.

Two sets of eyebrows shot up, and they did.

Another long, miserable silence was interrupted by a weird snorting noise. We all looked up.

The snorting was followed by a pounding stride.

"Did Toni just gain three hundred pounds?" Allison asked.

"Oh my God!" we all screamed at once.

Toni appeared from behind a bluff leading two mules. Make that three mules. Four.

We all screamed again.

Toni came toward us with a huge smile on her face. "Will you guys be quiet? You're going to scare them."

"Where did you find them?" Tommy asked.

Toni batted her eyelashes coyly. "I have my ways."

Allison groaned. "Oh no. You stole them."

Toni pretended to look insulted. "I did *not* steal them. I bargained for them."

Rosina looked suspicious. "Just what exactly did you bargain with?"

"Our Jeep."

"You sold our Jeep for four donkeys?" Rosina wailed.

Toni rolled her eyes. "Give me some credit, would you? We have a date to ride to South Rim Airport on Tuesday morning with four of the cutest guys you have ever seen in your life."

We named our mules first thing.

I mean, I'm sure they already had names, but we didn't know them, so we gave them new ones. Tommy rode Fleabag, Rosina rode Ugly, Allison rode Beavis, and since Toni and I are the lightest, we shared Butt-head.

Our proud and noble beasts weren't exactly fast, but it sure was easier having them do the climbing. And they climbed, all right. Straight up.

Best of all, they gave us the leisure to enjoy the most staggering views I have ever seen in my life.

The farther up we climbed, the more brilliant the sunset became. Fiery streaks of red, orange, gold, and violet painted the sky and illuminated dusky buttes, cliffs, and mesas for as far as the eye could see. Long after the vast, watery disk of sun disappeared into the depths of the canyon, the sky glowed with color. And the higher we climbed, the more of the incredible view was laid out before us.

I hated that river, but I had to admit it had carved a beautiful home for itself.

We were so awed by the sights, we just rode in a deep, peaceful silence, occasionally punctuated by a little sigh. No one even dug around for a camera. It was as though we all sensed that the magical night was too fragile and too wild ever to be held in the captivity of a picture frame.

The glow faded and the dark had transformed into shades of blue and purple long before we reached the rim. When at last we climbed out, we stopped to give our mules some water and a rest.

"Five minutes, and let's head home," Tommy said.

"Home?" I asked.

"Yeah. I figure we're staying at the grand Tilousi ranch tonight."

"We are?" Toni asked.

"Were you planning to stay at the Hilton?" Tommy asked.

Rosina's face turned hopeful. "Is there a Hilton?" she asked timidly.

We all started laughing.

"I think there's one in Flagstaff, but it will take Ugly at least a month to get there," Tommy told her.

Rosina frowned. "Very funny."

"How far is your ranch?" Allison asked.

"Um, let's see. Five minutes by car, fifteen minutes by foot, half-an-hour by mule."

"We're there," Toni said happily. She struggled to get back up on Butt-head for a few seconds, then turned around. Her face was pink. "Could, um, somebody give me a boost?"

My heart soared as we rode through the dark toward the bright lights of Tommy's ranch. It was a low, rambling wooden house, partially hidden by pine and cottonwood trees and surrounded by orchards and pastures. It was the most welcoming sight in the world.

A screen door slammed and someone came running toward us. Two people, actually. Tommy's parents? His brothers or sisters maybe?

I was thinking about how excited I was to meet his family when one of the faces suddenly came into the light.

"Debbie!" I shouted.

Toni shrieked and took a flying leap off Butt-head while he was going his full speed of three miles an hour. She practically tackled her sister in a hug. Debbie just laughed and hugged her back. Jim came running up right behind her. They both looked warmly dressed and happy.

We all pulled our mules to a stop and jumped off.

"How did you guys get here?" Allison asked.

"We thought you were shivering on the top of a cliff," I said.

"We were so worried," Allison said.

Toni put her hand on her hip. "Yeah, here we were scared to death. We're wet and freezing and covered with dirt, and you two are warm and dry and happy as clams."

Jim and Debbie looked at one another and smiled.

"We're sorry you worried," Jim said. "About an hour after you all had taken off down the river, we spotted a group of climbers at Dana Butte. They lent us gear and helped us climb up to the Tonto Plateau, and we hiked from there."

"But why did you come here?" Rosina asked.

"Because Tommy's house was close," Jim explained. "I've hung out at the Tilousi ranch hundreds of times."

Debbie laughed. "Come on, tell them the real reason."

Jim looked slightly sheepish. "Okay, okay. Mr. Tilousi is the best cook I have ever met."

That was when it occurred to me that I was absolutely starving. I felt like I hadn't eaten in years. My stomach let out a big rumble just to make sure I got the point. Being scared—I mean brave—really works up an appetite.

"And tonight is our lucky night," Debbie said. "Mr. Tilousi is making us a feast."

"Awesome," Allison declared.

"I'm so psyched," Rosina chimed in.

"Wait a minute," I said. "Before we do anything." I gestured to Tommy's makeshift splint. "He hurt his wrist. I'm worried it's broken."

Jim's face filled with alarm. "Oh no. Let me look."

Tommy shrugged. "It's not all that bad. Susette made me this awesome splint. The swelling has gone down a little."

"Let's go get your dad. He'll want somebody to take a look at it," Jim said, hustling Tommy into the house. We heard the screen door slam in the distance.

"Come on, let's get you all inside and warmed up," Debbie said, probably noticing that her sister was rapidly turning blue.

"What about John?" Toni asked, a little cloud passing over her face.

Debbie wrapped her jacket around Toni. "What about him?"

"We have to make sure he comes tonight. We can't have a feast without John," Allison said plaintively.

"It wouldn't be the same," I added. "I feel like we haven't seen him in ages."

Debbie frowned a little. "Well, it just so happens you're in luck," she said. "We already talked to John, and he's on his way over."

Did Debbie look disappointed when she said that? I wondered worriedly. Was she still really furious at John? Had she fallen for Jim? With all that had happened today, I had completely forgotten about Debbie and John, but now I was getting worried again.

More than ever I felt convinced of how important this summer was for all of us. What if Debbie stayed here with Jim and our whole adventure was over?

"Well, I'm glad he's coming," Toni said a little defiantly.

"Good for you." Debbie turned back toward the house. "I personally don't care if I see him for the rest of the summer," she muttered under her breath as she walked away, her hand in Jim's.

We all watched them in silence.

"Oh, no," Toni moaned.

Allison shook her head. "This doesn't look good."

"It looks awful," I agreed.

"Our plan was working, too," Toni said. "Darn it. We should never have let them get stuck on that rock together."

"Like we planned it," Rosina said wryly.

"What are we going to do?" I asked.

"We're not going to let this happen," Toni determined. "That's all there is to it."

Ten

"I can't put that underwear back on. Uh-uh. No way," Toni decided from where she lay in a fluffy terrycloth bathrobe on a big, comfortable bed piled high with down comforters and quilts.

After Mr. Tilousi had taken off with Tommy to the hospital, Mrs. Tilousi had shown us to this wonderful bedroom to shower and change. Like the rest of the house, it was simple but luxurious, with Native-American rugs and pottery decorating the rich dark wood of the floor and walls, and a fire crackling in the fireplace.

We had each taken a long hot shower and were now lounging around, sweet smelling and clean, in borrowed bathrobes.

"What about my T-shirt?" Rosina asked, crumpling up her face in disgust. "I can't put that back on."

"Have you checked out my socks?" Allison asked. "They should be in the corner, if they haven't gotten up and walked out of here yet."

I gazed morosely at the pile of damp, rumpled hiking shorts, T-shirts, bathing suit, and underwear lying beside the bed. My mother, by the way, would die if she saw me leave my clothes like that. "Putting dirty clothes on a clean body is truly a drag," I mused from my cozy spot on the floor in front of the fire.

"Could we just wear bathrobes to dinner?" Allison asked.

We all pondered that thought in silence for a few moments.

"Al, can I borrow your black-velvet leggings?" Toni asked out of the blue.

Allison stared at Toni in disbelief. "When?"

"Tonight."

Allison giggled. "Sure, Toni, no problem. Can I borrow your curling iron?"

"I don't have it with me," Toni said.

"And I don't have my velvet leggings with me, either," Allison replied.

"Yeah, you do."

Allison glared at Toni through narrowed eyes. "Toni, no offense, but did you smack your head on a rock today or something?"

"No," Toni said with a smug little smile.

"But John did just drive up in the Jeep with all our suitcases and stuff from the hotel."

"Ahhhhhhh!" Allison shouted.

I spun around to the window. Sure enough, there was John parking the Jeep, which was loaded high with suitcases.

We all jumped up and went flying out of the room. We practically flattened John on our way to the suitcases. Not that we weren't happy to see him, but the idea of clean clothes had never seemed so exciting. We thanked John, grabbed our suitcases, and hauled them into our room.

"Clean underwear!" Toni cried victoriously.

"I can't wait to put on my jeans," I said.

"I'm going to wear my pleated miniskirt," Rosina declared.

Suddenly, clothes were flying all over the room.

"Rosina, can I borrow your pink silk scrunchy?" Toni asked, running a brush through her long, unruly brown hair.

"Sure, if I can borrow your choker," Rosina said.

"That blouse is really cool," Allison said to Toni. I glanced over. It was really nice—this wispy black crepe material with big colorful flowers.

"What are you going to wear under it?" Allison asked.

Toni gave her most charming smile. "Your black-velvet leggings."

"What?" Allison demanded. "No way. I'm wearing those."

"But Al, you already said I could," Toni said with that devilish smile of hers.

Twenty minutes later the room looked like a typhoon had hit it, but we were dressed to kill. Or at least my friends were.

Rosina had on her pleated red mini with an ivory ruffled blouse and Toni's black braided choker.

Allison wore Toni's cropped red chenille sweater with slightly flared white jeans.

Toni wore her beautiful black floral blouse with—you guessed it—the velvet leggings.

And I wore Levi's and a blue turtleneck. So sue me. I'm not much of a fashion plate.

Suddenly I realized all my friends' eyes were on me, and it was making me a little uncomfortable.

"Um, Sus," Allison began tactfully, "did you bring any other shirts besides that turtleneck?"

"Yeah, and what about a little jewelry?" Toni suggested.

That was all it took. Minutes later all three of them were rifling through my suitcase. And by the looks on their faces, nothing they found there was quite right.

"You know what would look gorgeous on her?" Rosina asked, clearly in the midst of a major brainstorm. "Hang on." She started rooting through her own expansive leather suitcase. At last she found what she wanted: an emerald green washed silk tunic with delicate and beautiful beading around the neck and sleeves. When she held it up, I caught my breath. It was the most gorgeous piece of clothing I had ever seen.

"Wow," Toni said in awe.

"Amazing," Allison breathed.

"Try it on," Rosina said, shaking it at me impatiently.

"But I—I can't," I protested lamely. "It's too nice."

All three of them rolled their eyes at the same time. "That's ridiculous," Rosina informed me. "Try it on."

"Come on," Toni said excitedly. "You have to."

Slowly, reluctantly, I shed my turtleneck and pulled the soft material over my head. It settled over my body in a perfect fit. I looked up hesitantly.

"Ohhh," Allison said.

"You look beautiful," Toni said.

"It was made for you," Rosina said.

The three of them kept scrutinizing me.

"Hmmm," Toni said thoughtfully. "But you know what she needs?"

The other two nodded and sat me down on the bed.

Suddenly I was surrounded by brushes, hair mousse, eyeliners, lipgloss. I was ordered to look up, look down. Open my mouth, close my eyes.

I didn't even protest.

At last the three of them stood back, admiring their work. None of them said a thing. Toni just grabbed my hand and led me over to the mirror.

I stared at that person in the mirror for quite a while before I truly believed it was me. It's not that I didn't think I was pretty. But I just . . . I never, ever looked like this before. I looked older, glamorous, confident. Brave, even.

Then I was struck by a thought. My parents would have a heart attack if they saw me like this. They would be upset and disappointed, and my mother would demand that I go upstairs, wash my face, and change into something more sensible.

More than anything it was because the person in the mirror didn't look like their little girl anymore.

I studied the face in the mirror again. The face smiled at me. And I decided right then that no matter what my parents would say, I liked that person in the mirror. She was somebody I wanted to be.

"Something's still not quite right," Toni said, breaking my reverie.

"I know what you mean," Allison said, giving me another critical look.

Rosina looked from me to Toni and back again. "I think I know what it is."

Allison nodded. "Me, too."

Toni tapped her finger thoughtfully against her chin. "I'm afraid you're right, guys." She shimmied out of her leggings and held them out to me.

I gazed at her in astonishment. "No way, Toni. I don't need those. They look beautiful on you."

The three of them nodded again in agreement.

"Oh, come on," I said.

Toni shrugged. "Sorry. No choice. Put 'em on."

At last I gave in. I pulled off my jeans and pulled on the soft, plush leggings, while Toni unearthed her black jeans.

Rosina tossed a pair of velvet slippers at me, and the outfit was complete.

The three of them gave me a last long look, finally satisfied.

"Ready for dinner?" I asked sheepishly.

Allison smiled at me as we headed for the door. "Tommy Tilousi can kiss his poor heart good-bye."

The dining-room table was aglow with candles and set for twelve in colorfully painted pottery and woven placemats. Incredibly delicious smells wafted from the kitchen.

Mrs. Tilousi, Debbie, John, Jim, and a young woman I didn't recognize were already gathered around the table when we walked in.

"Well, don't you girls look beautiful," Mrs. Tilousi said.

"What a transformation," Debbie said.

"How's Tommy?" I asked Mrs. Tilousi worriedly. "Have you heard anything?"

Mrs. Tilousi put her arm around me. "His dad called a few minutes ago. He's fine. He's got a hairline fracture, so they set it in a cast. He'll be good as new in six weeks."

"They're on their way home right now," said the young woman I didn't recognize.

"Oh, girls, excuse me. I'd like to introduce you to my daughter, Maia," Mrs. Tilousi said, gesturing to her.

We all smiled and said hi. I should have guessed she was Tommy's sister. She had thick dark hair, high cheekbones, and a gorgeous smile, just like his. She looked as though she was around Debbie's age.

I was relieved that Tommy was okay, but as I thought of seeing him, I felt a flutter of nervousness in my stomach. What would he think when he saw me like this? Would he think I'd dressed up for him? Would he think I looked stupid, wearing clothes that weren't mine, pretending to be grown up?

I was on a roll. I had just barely begun to think of things to worry about when I looked up and saw that Tommy had come into the room, his arm covered in a cast and cradled in a splint. Our eyes met.

He looked a little surprised. But by the way his eyes lingered on mine, I don't think he thought I looked stupid.

I think he thought I looked nice.

At least I hoped so.

Eleven

"So I was leaning way out over the canyon wall when the rope broke," Debbie explained as she put her fork down. "I was pretty terrified."

I took another bite of the spicy corn salad Mr. Tilousi had made. All of us were gathered around the table, our plates heaped with the most delicious food you've ever tasted, telling the stories of our day. We were all flushed and warm from the heat of the fire in the fireplace.

"We were all terrified," Jim said. "I feel so awful about it."

Debbie put her hand on Jim's shoulder. "Please don't. It wasn't your fault."

Toni shot me a warning glance across the table. "Debbie was so brave," she said to John, who was sitting on her left. "You should have seen her."

"She really was," I chimed in.

John nodded. "I'm not at all surprised. I'm

so sorry for not going along with you today.
If I had any idea . . ." He broke off and
looked apologetically at Debbie. "If I had any
idea the kind of trouble you'd have . . ."

John really did look sorry. Earlier, when
we'd given him the quick version of our adventures, he'd turned several shades of
white.

"That's okay," Toni said. "Although Debbie—all of us—really missed you."

John gave a hesitant smile to Debbie.

This was clearly a point in our favor. John
felt bad and was trying to make it up to Debbie. She couldn't resist that, could she?

Debbie frowned at John and looked away.

I guess she could.

"I want to hear what happened to Tommy
and the girls after they left you on the rock,"
Mrs. Tilousi said.

Allison just shook her head and laughed.
"It was pretty ugly. We got on the raft, took
off through the most incredible field of rapids—"

"Horn Creek Rapids," Tommy supplied.
"The water was low, and the rapids were vicious."

"Yeah, we were thrown from one to the
next, crashing down and flying up again,"
Toni said, breaking off a piece of bread.

"Oh, no," Debbie said, putting her hand to her forehead. "I'm almost glad I didn't have to witness this."

"Just wait, it gets much worse," Rosina said.

"The rapids calmed down and we thought we were home free," Allison explained. "We all took a big breath of relief. And then we realized there was nothing ahead of us."

"What do you mean?" Maia asked.

"The water just dropped off into nothing."

"Waterfall?" Jim asked, cringing.

"It was a monster," Tommy said. "There must have been some kind of avalanche in Granite Gorge after the last big storm. A lot of rocks were dropped into the river, because the fall wasn't there the last time I ran that part of the river."

"We were heading straight for it and there was nothing we could do," I said. I felt my pulse racing with the memory.

"Oh, no," Debbie said.

"Oh, yes," Toni said, delighting in Debbie's anguish. "We went flying over it, soared high in the air, then . . ."

"Bam," Allison supplied.

I looked at the faces around the table, listening in suspense. Everyone had stopped eating.

"The raft landed hard, got caught under the fall and flipped," Tommy said.

"I can't even remember what happened after that," Rosina said. "All I know is, Toni, Allison, and I got carried down the river for what seemed like forever. Then we dragged ourselves up onto a bank. Toni caught the raft and dragged it up, too."

"Quick thinking, Toni," Jim said.

Toni shrugged modestly. "I know."

"What about Susette and Tommy?" John asked.

Tommy picked up his water glass. "Susette got caught in a whirlpool. It was a nightmare. I hauled her out of there just before she lost consciousness."

Debbie gasped. "Oh no."

John had his head in his hands. "Oh no."

"Your parents are going to die when they hear about this," Debbie groaned.

I cleared my throat. "That's why I kind of thought it might be better if we . . . um, gave them the edited version of the story." I gazed at them worriedly. I could practically see the conflict pass over John's face. He looked at Debbie for backup.

"Maybe we should, uh, let Susette tell them what happened," she said slowly. "After all, we weren't even there to see it."

I sighed in relief. I knew that meant it would be okay. Not that I was going to lie to my parents exactly. It's just that I might gloss over a few parts of the story.

"So what happened after the whirlpool?" Maia asked. "Is that when you hurt your wrist, Tommy?"

"Yeah, Susette and I hit a boulder pretty hard." He held up his cast. "It's fine now. Doesn't even hurt." He took a bite of black beans and rice. "Anyway, Susette and I swam to the shore after that. She made me a splint and put together this incredible raft in about five seconds flat."

"I was putting off the inevitable," I said. "I was terrified to get back in the water. I completely and totally panicked."

"You panicked?" Rosina asked, looking a little surprised. "You're always so cool, Sus."

Tommy and I just looked at each other and laughed.

After dinner, we all hung out around the fireplace in the Tilousis' sprawling living room, reading, drinking tea, talking.

Toni, Allison, Rosina, and I were talking with Jim and Debbie. Well, more precisely, Allison and Rosina were bugging Debbie as she tried to read her book, and Toni bothered Jim while he was trying to put waterproofing gunk on his boots. I sort of went back and forth keeping an eye on things—and, I admit, keeping an eye on Tommy, too.

"It's not Debbie's taste in music that gets to me," Toni was saying to Jim, tucking her feet under her on the couch. "I mean, Barry Manilow is fine if that's what you're into. It's the volume that gets me."

Jim looked up from his boots. "I thought you said she worships Axl Rose," he said, a tiny smile playing on his mouth.

Toni's face fell for a split second. "Axl Rose, Barry Manilow. Debbie loves 'em both," Toni said, recovering herself. "She's a weird girl, what can I say?"

This was too horrible. I grabbed my mug of tea and scooted over on the couch to where Debbie was sitting.

"I mean, I like Jim and everything," I overheard Allison telling her. "Hey, so what if he wheezes. We can't all have clear sinuses."

Debbie cocked her head to one side. "Allison, what are you talking about? Jim doesn't wheeze."

Rosina nodded confidently. "I sat next to him at dinner. Definite wheezing. Especially when his mouth was full."

"Come to think of it, he sort of chews with his mouth open, doesn't he?" Allison mused.

Debbie grimaced. "This is a very weird subject. Do you mind if I go back to my book?"

"Oh, sure. No problem," Allison said with a wave of her hand.

Debbie went back to her book.

"Now *John* has very clear sinuses," Allison added a few moments later.

"Allison."

"Sorry," Allison said.

I just rolled my eyes. At this rate Debbie really was going to bag the rest of our summer. And it wouldn't be because she hated John.

It would be because she couldn't stand *us*.

I was staring despondently into my cup of tea a few minutes later when Tommy came over and tapped my shoulder.

"Want to come take a walk with me?" he asked very quietly.

I felt my heart do a little flip-flop. "Um, sure," I said, hearing a little squeak in my voice.

I stood up, feeling everyone's eyes on my back as Tommy and I walked out the door.

The door slammed behind us and we

walked out into the cool, crisp night. Tommy reached out and held my hand as we passed under a canopy of trees.

I felt a tingle climb up my arm. It felt wonderful to have Tommy's fingers wrapped around mine. But what if my hand felt cold and clammy? What if my palms started sweating out of nervousness? What if I was holding his hand too tight? I immediately loosened my grip.

What if my hand felt like a dead fish? I tightened it again.

Relax, I commanded myself.

"What's the matter?" Tommy asked. "You looked sort of sad in there."

"Oh, we're a little worried about Debbie and John," I explained. "They don't seem to be getting along at all. And Debbie seems to be falling for Jim. It's none of our business, really . . ." I smiled ruefully. "But that's never stopped us before. And the thing is, if Debbie really is that mad at John, and if she decides to spend the rest of the summer here with Jim, our whole trip will be over."

Tommy shook his head and laughed. "This is confusing."

"I know."

He thought about it for a second. "Okay, so you're worried that Jim and Debbie are

getting together, and that she's going to stay
here for the summer."

"Right."

"That doesn't sound so bad." He stopped
walking and looked at me. "Maybe you could
stay, too?"

He had the nicest, most sincere look in his
eyes. It made me want to stay with him all
summer. I couldn't even reply.

"You can't, I know," he said finally.

He started leading me around to the
property behind the house. "I want to show
you my favorite place in the world," he told
me.

We walked through a meadow, climbed over
a fence. The moon was so big and high in
the night sky, we could see our shadows.

"Here," he said as we reached a long
stretch of an old stone wall. It was craggy and
overgrown, and somehow so romantic looking.
He held his good arm out toward me. "Want
a boost?"

I put my foot in his hand, hoping nervously
that I didn't feel like an elephant as I hoisted
myself onto the wall. I turned around and sat
down.

That's when I realized why he loved this
place. From my perch on the wall, I could
see the canyon spreading out for miles and

miles. The river at the bottom looked like nothing more than a trickle from up here.

Tommy climbed up beside me and took my hand again.

"This is so beautiful," I said.

"I think so, too," he said.

We just sat there in silence, watching the moon rise over the canyon.

"You didn't like me much when we first met, did you?" Tommy asked.

I laughed. "Nope."

He laughed, too. "I guess I was kind of a pain in the butt."

"Yep."

Tommy put a foot up on the wall. "From the second I first saw you, you made me nervous. I don't handle being nervous well."

I laughed again. "That makes two of us."

"Do you like me a little better now?" he asked, staring down at his hands.

"A lot."

He smiled his gorgeous, drop-dead smile. "I'm glad."

"I . . . have trouble trusting people sometimes," I said. "After what happened to us on the river today, though, I trust you."

"I trust you, too."

"Thanks," I said.

We were quiet again. I felt as if all the

nerves in my body were concentrated into my hand that was wrapped in his.

"Hey, look," he said, turning his face upward.

I looked up and caught my breath. "Wow," I breathed. The night sky pulsed with a million stars. It was the clearest, most perfect sky I'd ever seen.

As I stared up, hypnotized by the sky, I felt Tommy studying the side of my face.

"You look beautiful tonight," he said softly.

I turned to him. I expected my face to flush purple. My hands to start shaking. My heart to start thundering in my chest. But none of that happened. I smiled and said thank you.

Well, actually my heart was pounding. And it grew louder as he leaned toward me slowly, and his lips met mine.

My first kiss.

I didn't drown. I didn't faint. I kissed him back, and it felt wonderful.

Twelve

"He kissed you? Oh my God!" Toni shrieked, hugging me impulsively.

"Shhh," I commanded her, trying to look serious, but totally unable to wipe the smile off my face.

I had snuck quietly back into our room, tiptoed in, and all three of my friends pounced. So much for sneaking.

They all demanded to know *exactly* what had happened with Tommy. Every nanosecond.

So I told them. Although I did leave out a few nanoseconds.

"That is soooo romantic," Allison said.

"On the mouth?" Toni wanted to know.

I nodded.

"Of course on the mouth," Allison said, rolling her eyes at Toni.

I could tell Toni wished she hadn't asked that. She pretends to be very knowledgeable about boys, but I suspect she hasn't had much more experience than I have—except for a pretty serious crush on Paul, the guy we met on Whistler Mountain.

"Your first kiss, that's so cute," Rosina said.

"So tell me how it felt. Tell me everything," Toni demanded.

I glanced toward the door. "You guys, be quiet," I whispered. "It's late and we're supposed to be asleep."

"This is *important*," Toni wailed.

I sat down on the bed, my head still spinning. "It felt amazing," I said simply. "One second we were sitting together on a wall, and the next second we were kissing."

Toni and Allison sighed.

"It only lasted a few seconds," I said. "After we broke apart, we jumped down from the wall. We walked back to the house holding hands, hardly saying anything. I kept expecting to feel really awkward, but I didn't. I felt wonderful. Every few feet we'd turn to look at each other and just smile these big goofy smiles." I giggled. "We must have looked like such morons."

All three of them sighed.

"You're so lucky," Allison said.

"Tommy is so cute," Toni said.

"You make such a good couple," Rosina said.

I just smiled and flopped back on the bed. This was the most wonderful day of my whole life.

We were still chattering and getting ready for bed a few minutes later when we heard voices outside our door. We didn't pay much attention at first, until the voices rose a little, and we realized it was Jim and Debbie.

"Shhh," Toni said, hustling over to the door. Her eyes opened wide and she gestured for all of us to come over.

We all gathered around the door, straining to hear the voices.

"I can't stand to be away from you, either." It was Debbie's voice, full of emotion.

"Then stay. Please stay," Jim begged.

We all pressed closer against the door. My chin was on Allison's shoulder, Rosina's elbow was in my ribs.

"I don't know if I can," Debbie said.

"They have a place for you in the rafting company. I organized everything," Jim said. "The pay isn't great, but it isn't bad. And we'll be together," he added in a low voice.

We all turned and stared at one another in horror.

Oh, no, I thought worriedly. The thing we were most scared of was coming true.

"That would be so wonderful," Debbie whispered. "But what about my responsibilities? What about my sister, Allison, Susette, and Rosina?" she asked plaintively. "I don't want to disappoint them."

Toni was nodding grimly.

"Oh, they'll get over it," Jim said. "Besides, they've gotten so weird lately—"

He broke off, and I heard a little sniffling sound.

Was he crying? Was Debbie crying?

This was terrible.

"I can't believe they told you about my tapeworm," Debbie said in a trembling voice. "How did they find out?"

Toni's eyes grew round in shock.

I heard more sniffling noises.

"After all the strange things they've done . . . well, maybe you're right," Debbie continued. "Maybe I really should stay here. After all, who wants to spend the summer with four obnoxious little girls?"

All four of our faces fell in outrage. *Obnoxious little girls?*

At that second, the door opened. We were all squeezed up against it so hard, we collapsed on the floor in a pile. Someone switched a light on, and we all lay there blinking in astonishment.

That's when I heard it.

Laughter.

It was embarrassing, humiliating, and terrible.

Debbie, Jim, and John were standing in the hallway, looking at us and laughing their heads off.

"I've never felt so stupid in my entire life," Toni said, climbing under the covers. "And I've felt pretty stupid a few times."

Allison groaned. "They got us. They really did. How could we have fallen for that?"

"We're total losers," Rosina said grimly.

"Can you believe Maia turned out to be Jim's girlfriend?" I said, shaking my head. "Tommy must have thought I was completely nuts." I inched my sleeping bag a little closer to the fire. We'd drawn straws for the bed, and Toni and Rosina had won. Allison and I were in big, fluffy down sleeping bags on the floor.

"We have to leave Debbie and John alone after this," Allison resolved. "We can't bug them and we can't worry about them."

I nodded. "They may love each other and

they may hate each other, and it's none of our business," I said firmly.

"I don't even *care* what happens to them anymore," Toni declared. "We've got better things to think about."

"Definitely," Rosina said.

We all nodded and settled into our beds.

Suddenly Allison sat up in her sleeping bag. "What was that?" she asked, glancing out the window.

"What was what?" Toni asked.

Allison crawled out of her sleeping bag and went over to the window. "I heard something." She scanned the yard. "Turn the lamp off," she commanded Rosina.

Rosina flicked it off.

Allison gasped. "It's Debbie and John. They're standing together under a tree."

In a stampede, the other three of us rushed over to the window and pressed our faces against the glass.

John and Debbie were talking, their heads close together. We couldn't hear what they were saying, but John said something that made Debbie laugh.

I found a smile had crept onto my face. I wasn't the only one. Toni, Allison, and Rosina were watching every move excitedly.

As we watched in utter amazement, John leaned down and kissed Debbie.

"Oh my God!" Toni cried.

"No way!" Allison shrieked.

"I can't believe it," Rosina whispered.

The four of us turned to one another with huge grins on our faces. We all smacked each other's hands in a group high five.

"Yessss," Toni declared.

Debbie and John walked back toward the house, and all of us went back to our beds.

"We don't care what happens to Debbie and John," Allison said as she crept into her sleeping bag. "I don't care. Do you care?"

"Me?" Toni asked in mock surprise. "Couldn't care less."

"I certainly don't care," I chimed in, my heart soaring.

Thirteen

Saying good-bye to Tommy was the hardest thing. I saved it until the car was all packed up, and we absolutely positively had to go.

We were driving that morning to do a few days of easy hiking on the heavily wooded north rim of the canyon. Then we were packing up again and driving to Phoenix, where we were catching a flight to Boston and then on to Portland, Maine, where we'd start the third leg of our adventure—a sailing trip through the thousands of islands dotting Maine's rugged coastline.

John started up the car, we all said good-bye to Jim and thanked the Tilousis. Tommy gestured to me, and I followed him a little ways away, behind the garage.

He took my hand. "I wish we didn't have to say good-bye," he said.

I just nodded, not quite trusting my voice to speak.

"It's been an intense couple of days."

"It has," I said in a slightly wobbly voice.

"You are one of the bravest people I've met. Don't forget that," he said.

"I won't," I said. "Thank you."

"Thanks for what?" he asked.

"Thanks for . . ." Thanks for letting me trust you? For making me feel so good about myself? For being so unbelievably cute? ". . . for making me feel brave," I finished.

"That's not me," he said. "That's you."

"Well, then thanks for making me understand that," I said.

"Write to me, okay?" he asked.

"I promise," I said.

He leaned close and kissed me again.

We broke apart, and I started to walk away.

"Come back next summer?" he said after me. "I'll teach you how to swim."

I turned around and smiled. "I'd love that."

Then I walked across the yard and to the waiting car, knowing I would never forget him as long as I lived.

"And I-I-I-I-I will always love you-ou-ou-ou-ou-ou-ou-ou!"

"Toni, will you shut up!"

"All of you, be quiet," Debbie commanded. "Do I really have to spend the next two hours in the car with you?"

"Yep," Toni said happily.

I just sat back in my seat and smiled. As much as I was already missing Tommy, I was happy that our little traveling group was all together again, arguing, bickering, singing annoying songs, heading off to our next adventure.

If I learned as much on every one of our trips as I learned on this one, I would pretty much have the world figured out by September. Maybe I could just skip ninth grade. Maybe high school altogether. I could go straight to being a doctor or something, like that kid on TV.

As I watched the fierce Colorado River recede out of my window, I gave it a cocky stare. I remembered how I'd felt when I saw it the first time: awed by the beauty of the canyon it had made for itself, but scared to death of the power of the water.

But I had been through it. It had given me its worst and I'd survived. And in the meantime I learned to trust somebody with my fears. An incredibly cute somebody. An incredibly cute somebody who became my first sort-of boyfriend.

I felt as though I had finally put Thunder Lake behind me. Water wasn't going to scare me anymore.

I'd put those fears behind me once and for all.

"I once went sailing in a thunderstorm." Rosina's voice broke through my thoughts. "Totally terrifying," she was saying. "I've heard the weather in Maine is very unpredictable."

"My dad said he saw a whale off the coast of Maine once," Allison said.

"My cousin Jed lives in Bangor, and he says he sees sharks around there all the time," Toni said.

I sat up a little straighter, hearing the dull thud of my heart. Thunderstorms? Whales? Sharks?

Okay, so maybe I hadn't put all those fears behind me.

I was going to get a chance to be brave again.

Dear Grandpa,

I wish I could put into words everything I've seen and experienced. I know I can't. Maybe I'll write about it someday.

I made a new friend here. Somebody I

can talk to almost like I can talk to you. His name is Tommy and I think you'd like him a lot. He was our guide on the river-rafting trip. I got myself into some trouble in the river and was too scared to get back into the water after that. I told him I was scared, and he didn't laugh or tell me I was being stupid, like I expected. He told me only people who have fears are truly brave.

So anyway, unlike that time at camp, I got back into the water. I faced it again. And I felt so proud of myself.

I've grown up a lot on this trip. I'm not feeling so much like your little girl anymore, but I hope I'm becoming a young woman you'll be proud of.

Love,
Susette

Dear Readers:

Welcome back to *Adventurers, Inc.!*

If you look in the back of this book, you'll see a picture of me rock climbing. The story behind that photo is really cool.

I was in Vancouver and wanted to learn how to rock climb. It was raining, like usual in Vancouver, so I called an indoor rock-climbing place called The Edge and arranged for a lesson. (I think a lesson is the only place to start when it's a dangerous sport.)

They gave me special shoes and a harness and then introduced me to my instructor—a sixteen-year-old girl named Catherine! Well, I was shocked! Somehow I figured that if someone was going to be the only thing keeping me from crashing forty feet to the ground, that someone would be a big burly guy. Then I started to laugh, 'cause the whole point of these books is that girls, even small ones, can do *anything!* It's not size or sex that counts, but guts!

Well, Catherine was terrific. She showed me how to use my feet for leverage and my hands for lifting, how to tie the ropes—everything! I got scared about halfway up, but with her encouragement, I pushed through it and got to the top. She even relayed me down a huge wall. (It seemed huge to *me*, anyhow. She climbs walls that are even higher!)

I'm not sure I'm going to take up outdoor rock climbing (like Rosina, I find the "great outdoors" a little dirty for my taste—plus, where do you go to the bathroom while climbing a cliff?), but I know I'll be back to The Edge for another lesson. I just hope Catherine is available to teach me!

Please write soon. I can't wait to hear about your adventures!

Love,

Mally

Mallory

Write to Mallory c/o Elise Donner, Executive Editor, Z*Fave Books, Kensington Publishing Corporation, 850 Third Avenue, 16th Floor, New York, NY 10022.